The Clue of the Gold Doubloons

When Nancy reached the dressing room, she went straight to where Karl had hung his street clothes. She lifted his shirt off the peg. His buttons might have a partial fingerprint, but he was bound to notice if his shirt was missing.

Next she checked his jeans, rifling the pockets, hoping to find spare change, a comb, anything that might hold a print. They were empty.

Nancy blew out a frustrated breath. Her gaze landed on his belt. Of course! The metal buckle would be a perfect place to find a print.

Careful not to touch the buckle, Nancy began to pull the belt from the loops. The squeak of a floorboard made her glance over her shoulder.

Karl Kidd filled the dressing room doorway, a murderous expression on his face. Without a word, he raised his hand and hurled a dagger straight at Nancy's head!

Nancy Drew
Mystery Stories

Available from MINSTREL Books

NANCY DREW® 149

THE CLUE OF THE GOLD DOUBLOONS

CAROLYN KEENE

A MINSTREL® BOOK

Published by POCKET BOOKS
New York   London   Toronto   Sydney   Tokyo   Singapore

1476964

This book is a work of fiction. Names, characters, places and incidents are products of the author's imagination or are used fictitiously. Any resemblance to actual events or locales or persons living or dead is entirely coincidental.

A MINSTREL PAPERBACK *Original*

A Minstrel Book published by
POCKET BOOKS, a division of Simon & Schuster Inc.
1230 Avenue of the Americas, New York, NY 10020

Copyright © 1999 by Simon & Schuster Inc.

ISBN: 0-671-02548-1

First Minstrel Books printing May 1999

10 9 8 7 6 5 4 3

NANCY DREW, NANCY DREW MYSTERY STORIES, A MINSTREL BOOK and colophon are registered trademarks of Simon & Schuster, Inc.

Cover art by Ernie Norcia

Printed in the U.S.A.

Contents

1

City of Pirates

"I love the Inner Harbor," Nancy Drew announced as she and her friend George Fayne strolled along the bustling brick walkway that surrounded Baltimore's Patapsco River.

"I agree," George said. An Orioles baseball cap covered her curly brown hair, and the two girls were dressed for the warm weather in shorts, tennis shoes, and T-shirts.

It was a gorgeous September Monday. The sun sparkled off the water, and a breeze ruffled Nancy's reddish blond hair. Tour boats were docked along the wharf area, and small pleasure boats dotted the river.

"I'm dying to spend some time sightseeing," Nancy said.

George laughed. "I don't think we're going to have much time to sightsee. Andrew, Daniel, and their film will keep us plenty busy."

"True." Nancy stopped to watch a juggler toss balls into the air. The Inner Harbor was crowded with tourists visiting one of Baltimore's biggest attractions. The harbor had once been a polluted industrial area. Now it was a 240-acre complex of museums, interesting shops, excellent restaurants, and high-tech offices.

"Andrew's determined to keep on schedule," Nancy added as they continued on their way. "He says we'll be finished filming in a week. Maybe we'll have some free time then."

Andrew and Daniel Wagner were the twenty-four-year-old owners of the fledgling film company Seeing Double Productions. During the summer, George and Nancy had taken a film-making course. The twin brothers had taught one of the workshops. After the course ended, Nancy and George had talked to them. They'd discovered the twins were working on a documentary about pirates. Nancy had been intrigued with the subject as well as with filmmaking.

She and George had volunteered to join the small group, first helping to write the documentary. When the script for *Robbers of the High Seas* was finished, George was chosen to play the part of Anne Bonny, a famous eighteenth-century female pirate. Nancy had enjoyed the more technical side, so Andrew had enlisted her as his assistant director.

"Too bad Bess couldn't be here," George said when they passed Harborplace, two glass-enclosed pavilions filled with shops and restaurants.

Bess had just started a part-time job and didn't want to leave River Heights.

"Maybe it's good she's not here," Nancy said jokingly. "We might find out the real meaning of 'shop until you drop.'"

"So where is the *Swift Adventure?*" George asked.

Nancy pulled out a travel brochure. "Pier Three. If I remember correctly, the aquarium is on the other side of the Trade Center. The Maritime Museum is beyond that, and that's where the *Swift Adventure* is docked."

A week earlier Andrew had received permission to use the *Swift Adventure* to film many of the scenes. To save money, the two brothers were also staying on the ship.

Earlier Nancy and George had checked into the Harborside Hotel. Selena Ramirez, the only professional actress hired to be in the documentary, was also staying at the Harborside.

Nancy wasn't sure where the rest of the cast and crew were bunking. In fact, she wasn't sure who the rest of the cast and the crew were. All she knew was that a group had arrived two days earlier to prepare the ship for filming.

When she and George reached the other side of the Trade Center, Nancy spotted three tall masts. "We must be headed in the right direction," she said.

"I hope we get to see the aquarium again," George said when they passed the unusual buildings that housed more than six hundred different types of sea creatures. "Last time we were here, we were too busy with a case to see all the animals."

"Let's put it at the top of our sight-seeing list," Nancy agreed. Seconds later the two girls crossed a wooden bridge to Pier Three.

"There's the ship." Stopping on the pier, Nancy tilted her head back to check out the *Swift Adventure*, a square-rigged galley that had been built in the early 1700s. It had three tall masts. The sails were unfurled and tied back so that the complicated system of masts, yards, ladders, and rigging was exposed.

While working on the script, Nancy and George had researched seventeenth- and eighteenth-century ships. They had learned that pirates captured or stole many kinds of boats but preferred small, fast vessels, like galleys, that could overtake the heavier cargo ships.

George gave a low whistle. "The ship's perfect for the film. I'm so glad the twins are getting to use it."

"They're paying for the use," Nancy reminded

her friend. "The historical society that maintains it is charging a pretty hefty fee."

Just then a round, pixieish face peered over the edge of the ship's railing. Nancy waved.

"It's Janie!" Nancy told George, referring to Janie Simms, the film's production manager. The petite brunette had been with the project from the very beginning, raising money, scheduling filming, and locating equipment.

Janie waved back. "Ahoy, mates!"

Nancy grinned, then hurried after George, who was heading up the pier to the gangplank. A group of tourists was converging on the ship from the other direction.

"The *Swift Adventure* is being used to film *Robbers of the High Seas*," a guide was saying as he led the group up the gangplank. "We may still tour parts of the ship, but please stay on the outside of the ropes so we don't disturb the film crew."

George shot Nancy a puzzled look. "I didn't realize we were going to have spectators," she whispered as they followed the group up the gangplank to the waist of the ship, which was the lower area between the foredeck and the quarterdeck.

Chattering excitedly, the tourists followed their guide toward the foredeck. Nancy and George headed to the stern. Stepping over the low rope, they climbed up the ladder to the raised quarterdeck, which was filled with milling people. Some carried equipment. Some were setting up lights and cameras.

Nancy recognized several people. There was Harold Oates, who had taught one of their classes on lighting and sound, and Lian Chu, a cameraperson. Nancy also spotted Janie, who was intently discussing something with a pretty woman with long jet-black hair.

"There're Andrew and Daniel," George said, pointing to the middle of the quarterdeck. "We'd better ask them what they want us to do."

The twins were standing beside the towering mizzenmast. Daniel was waving something in the air. Andrew had his fists planted on his hips. Nancy couldn't hear what the brothers were saying, but from their gestures, she could tell they were arguing.

"I guess we'd better check in," Nancy said. "Though it looks as if they're having one of their 'artistic disagreements.'"

When they'd worked with the twins on the script, Nancy and George had quickly learned that even though Daniel and Andrew were identical in looks, their personalities were quite different.

Daniel was an actor. He was going to play a character named Calico Jack Rackham in the film. He usually spoke in a booming voice accompanied by dramatic hand gestures, as if he were always onstage. He wore loose-fitting Hawaiian-print shirts, sandals, and baggy shorts. His brown hair was pulled back into a short ponytail, and a gold earring glittered in one earlobe.

Andrew got more involved in the business end of filmmaking, and he tended to worry about practical matters. He usually wore polo shirts, tailored slacks, and deck shoes. His hair was trimmed neatly around his ears. He kept several pens in his shirt pocket, and this afternoon he carried a clipboard thick with papers.

As Nancy drew nearer, she could clearly hear what the twins were saying. "I refuse to use this musket!" Daniel was shouting. "It looks like Eli bought it at a toy store."

"That's because he *did* buy it at a toy store," Andrew shouted back. "For five bucks. A replica from the Prop Shop costs fifty dollars. No one watching the film will know the difference."

Cupping her hand around one side of her mouth, George whispered to Nancy, "Do you get the feeling our ship isn't so shipshape?"

Suddenly, Andrew spotted them. "Nancy! George!" He waved them over. "Am I glad you finally made it. We need some sanity around here." He flung an arm around Nancy's shoulder. "Nancy, tell Daniel I cannot afford museum-quality props."

"George." Daniel put his arm around George's shoulder. "Tell Andrew if he wants this film to look authentic, he can't use props from a toy store."

"Uh," George began. She glanced at Nancy, and the two started laughing.

With a look of pretend disgust, Andrew smacked his clipboard against his thigh. "Even my assistant director doesn't take me seriously." Then he smiled and gave Nancy's shoulder a squeeze. "Glad you're here. This place is a zoo!"

"What can we do to help?" Nancy asked.

Andrew pulled a piece of paper from his clipboard. "Here's a list to get you started. George, you—"

"Oh no, George is *mine*," Daniel stated firmly. "I'm taking her below-decks to get her fitted into her costume." Furrowing his brow, he frowned at George. "Have you got your lines ready, Anne Bonny?"

" 'If there's a man among ye, ye'll come out and fight like the men ye are to be,' " George recited.

Nancy laughed. "She's been practicing ever since we left River Heights."

"Great!" Daniel beamed at George. "I'll introduce you to Eli Wakefield, who's in charge of costumes as well as props." He shot Andrew a disgusted look. "Eli does a great job, considering the stingy budget he's got to work with."

"We're lucky there's any money left in the budget," Andrew retorted, "after you ordered those so-called authentic gold doubloons, which cost a fortune."

That set them off again, giving Nancy a chance to glance at her list. There were at least twenty things she was supposed to do.

"Daniel!" A gruff voice broke into Nancy's thoughts. A huge grizzly bear of a guy was striding toward them. With his pitch-black beard, bushy brows, and scraggly long hair, he looked like a real pirate.

"What's with this script?" the guy said, smacking some rolled-up papers against his palm. "You've turned Blackbeard into a wimp!"

"Karl, the documentary is partially funded by educational television," Daniel explained. "We're hoping it will be shown in schools all over the United States. We had to keep it clean."

Karl snorted. "Clean? This has been positively *sanitized.*" Unrolling the papers, he read, " 'Pirates, prepare for battle.' That sounds like somebody's granny talking. Not the fearsome—"

"Nancy." Andrew steered Nancy away from Daniel and Karl. "Ignore those two. First thing you need to do is help Janie with Selena."

Nancy glanced over at the two women, who were standing at the railing of the stern. The dark-skinned woman with Janie was gorgeous. Her short-shorts, platform sandals, and halter top accented her long legs and curvaceous figure, and her waist-length hair gleamed like polished ebony.

"Selena is turning into a major problem." Andrew rolled his eyes. "I just hope hiring her is worth the aggravation and money. Anyway, Janie's about had it with Selena's demands. Maybe you can smooth things over."

"How am I supposed to—" Nancy began, but Andrew was striding away, hollering to a woman laying a sheet of plywood on the deck. "Lian! Don't put that camera track there. We're shooting on the starboard side."

For a second Nancy pressed her fingertips to her forehead. The place *was* a zoo.

"Men's clothes! You've got to be kidding!" A shrill voice made Nancy turn her attention back to Janie and Selena. "You want to hide this work of art in baggy pants and shirt?" Spreading her arms wide, the actress twirled in a circle. Instantly, several guys stopped what they were doing to stare.

Nancy glanced at Janie, whose face was flushed red. Andrew was right, Nancy thought. The production manager looked as if she were ready to explode.

Plastering a welcoming smile on her face, Nancy rushed over, her hand outstretched. "Selena, I'm Nancy Drew, the assistant director." She pumped the woman's arm. "I couldn't help overhearing your complaint, and I want to say that your acting will be so fantastic, *every* director will notice you."

Selena arched her perfectly plucked brows. "Hmm. You have a point, Ms. Drew. A dynamite body and an award-winning performance. A deadly combination."

"Deadly," Janie echoed, flashing Nancy a smile of thanks.

10

Just then someone jostled Nancy.

"Sorry. Sorry." Smiling apologetically, Harold Oates bustled past carrying a shotgun microphone. Harold was as tall and gangly as a giraffe, and with the long microphone in his arms, he appeared even more awkward.

Suddenly, someone yelled, "Heads up!"

Snapping her head back, Nancy looked skyward. A heavy coil of rope was hurtling toward deck—straight for Harold Oates.

"Harold, get out of the way!" she cried.

Startled, Harold glanced up. When he saw the rope, he raised one arm to shield his face. The long microphone tipped sideways, throwing him off balance, and he fell against the wooden railing.

With a loud crack, the railing broke. Nancy tried to grab him, but she wasn't fast enough. Arms flailing, Harold toppled through the broken railing, landing with a splash in the muddy water below.

2

A Golden Clue

Nancy rushed to the broken railing. The brown water closed over Harold, and he disappeared from her view.

"He can't swim!" Janie shouted in Nancy's ear. By now several crew members had run over to the railing.

Nancy searched for signs of Harold in the water, but it was as if the muddy river had swallowed him. Without hesitating, she stuck her list of chores in her pocket and kicked off her tennis shoes. "I'm going in after him."

"No!" Janie grabbed her arm. "It's too dangerous."

"We don't have any choice," Nancy cried. "Harold may have bumped his head or injured himself. We don't have time to run off the ship to the wharf."

Taking a breath, she peered over the side of the ship. It was about twenty feet to the water.

Not much higher than a high diving board, Nancy thought. Before anyone could stop her, she stepped over the broken railing and jumped feet first, landing with her arms outstretched to keep from plunging too deep. Still, the cold water closed over her like a black curtain. Immediately, she brought her arms down to her sides and kicked hard, breaking the surface.

When she looked around, she couldn't tell where Harold had fallen in.

"Nancy! There are bubbles to your left!" Janie called from the deck above.

Nancy swam to the spot where Janie was pointing. She swept her arms through the water and connected with something solid. It was Harold's arm. Grasping it, she pulled. Slowly, he came to the surface. His skin was blue, but when his head popped above water, he began to gasp for air.

Just then someone came swimming around the stern of the boat. When the person drew closer, Nancy recognized Karl, the Blackbeard actor.

"I'll tow him in!" Karl called. Grabbing Harold in a lifesaving hold, he swam toward the pier. Nancy followed. A curious throng stared at them from the pier.

When Nancy reached the side of the pier, several people reached down to pull her up.

Janie rushed over, a towel in her hand. "Are you all right?" When Nancy nodded, Janie draped the towel over her shoulders.

As she dried her face, Nancy glanced around. "Where are Karl and Harold?"

"Over here." Saying "Excuse me, excuse me," Janie led Nancy through the crowd. Karl had laid Harold down and was kneeling next to him. He was bending over to perform mouth-to-mouth resuscitation when Harold pushed him away. "Get out of here, you big gorilla, I'm fine!"

Coughing and sputtering, Harold sat up. His hair was plastered to his head, and his skin was tinged with grime.

"Should we call the rescue squad?" Janie asked. "You don't look so hot."

Harold shivered. "I'm fine. When I went under I swallowed a mouthful of water. Then I panicked and got disoriented. The water was so muddy I couldn't see anything. Then I felt someone grab my arm. Karl, was that you?"

"Nope. It was our new assistant director, Nancy Drew." Grinning, he waved at Nancy. "For once Andrew has done something right. He hired someone with guts."

"And someone who could swim," Harold added grimly. "Thank you, Nancy."

"Let me through. Let me through!" a voice called, and a second later, Andrew pushed past Nancy and squatted next to Harold. "Hey, buddy, is my best sound and light man all right?"

Harold gave him a weak grin. "Yeah, I'm okay. Thanks to your assistant. A hot shower and dry clothes and I'll be as good as new."

"Great." With a worried expression, Andrew glanced around. "Where's the microphone?"

"Microphone?" Harold stared at him.

"Yeah. The shotgun microphone you were holding when you went overboard." When Harold didn't respond, Andrew looked up at Nancy.

"I didn't see the microphone," she said. "It must have gone under."

"Karl? Did you see it?" Andrew asked anxiously.

"Nope. I was too busy pulling Harold in."

"Oh, great." With a groan of dismay, Andrew clapped a hand to his head. "It was brand-new! Somebody needs to jump in and find it."

For a second Nancy wasn't sure she'd heard him correctly. She glanced over at Janie, Harold, and Karl, and saw that they looked just as surprised.

Finally Harold said, "I guess it'll have to be you, Andrew. Nobody else is crazy enough to dive in on purpose. Plus, the water's so muddy, you'd never find the microphone."

15

"Well, that's just terrific." Andrew jumped up. "One more problem to add to my list of headaches," he said before stomping off.

"What was that all about?" Karl asked.

Janie sighed. "He's under a lot of pressure."

Harold snorted. "He was more worried about the microphone than he was about me."

Nancy turned to Karl. Water dripped off his brows and mustache. "Thanks for towing Harold in."

"My pleasure. I'm Karl Kidd, by the way." Grabbing her hand with a huge paw, he shook it so hard Nancy winced. "Otherwise known as Blackbeard."

"And I'm Harold, soaking wet," Harold announced as he stood up.

"Well, forget the hot shower and dry clothes," Janie said. "Andrew plans to block scene three in ten minutes. He wants everybody there. And you know how he is about keeping to the schedule."

"But I'm wet and cold!" Harold protested.

Pulling the towel from her shoulder, Nancy handed it to Harold. "Use this. The sun's so warm, we'll be dry in a minute."

When the four started back to the ship, Karl asked, "So what happened, Harold? Were you practicing for your big 'man overboard' scene?"

"Very funny, Kidd. Actually, I'm not sure what happened."

"A coil of rope fell from one of the masts,"

Nancy explained. "Fortunately, someone yelled 'heads up' before you were hit."

"That was Lian," Janie said. "Lucky she saw the rope fall."

"A rope, huh?" Stopping at the bottom of the gangplank, Karl wiggled his thick brows. "Someone out to get you, Oates? A jealous girlfriend?"

Harold rolled his eyes. "Yeah, right. I'm such a lady-killer."

As Nancy followed them up, she suddenly realized that everything had happened so quickly, she hadn't even thought about the falling rope. Was it possible that someone *had* deliberately dropped it? she wondered.

When she reached the ship's deck, Nancy stopped to let the others go ahead. Shielding her eyes with her hand, she stared up at the mizzenmast. It was a web of sails, yards, and rigging. Nancy knew from her research that sailors used the rope ratlines as ladders to climb from the lower masts to the top masts.

In the confusion, someone could have clambered up or down the ratlines without anyone noticing. But why would someone want to hurt Harold? Nancy thought.

"Where's my assistant director?" A loud voice boomed over the ship. Nancy recognized Andrew's bellow. When she went up the steps to the quarterdeck, she saw the cast and crew gathering on the starboard side of the stern.

Selena, George, and Daniel, who were the actors in scene three, stood by the railing in their regular clothes. Karl and Janie and Harold were standing on the sidelines. Harold had gone over to get another microphone. A camera and several lights had been set up.

Tucking her damp hair behind her ears, Nancy hurried over. She stuck her hand in her shorts pocket. Her list of things to do was soaked, but from the impatient expression on Andrew's face, she realized she wouldn't have time to work on it anyway.

When she reached Andrew, he thrust a roll of masking tape into her hands. "We're blocking scene three. You're in charge of taping the actors' marks."

Nancy nodded. "Blocking a scene" meant the director and cameraperson figured out the best camera shots.

"For the beginning of this scene, Daniel and George will face each other," Andrew instructed. "Selena, you lean on the railing, staring out to sea."

"But my back will be turned to the audience!" Selena protested.

"Fortunately, you have a gorgeous back. Lian, how do you think that will look?" Andrew asked, ignoring Selena's frown of displeasure.

Lian was sitting behind the camera. Because of

the uneven surface of the deck, the camera's wheels had been mounted on a track on the plywood. "It looks great," she said. "Let me try a close-up next."

Andrew pointed to Selena's sandaled feet. "Nancy, put tape on the board right here," he instructed. "And over here—"

Nancy hustled forward. Actors' marks let the actors know where to stand during a scene and were used to keep track of the blocking. The characters in movies might act naturally, but Nancy had learned from her filmmaking course that every move was carefully planned. For each scene, a few different angles were shot. When it was edited later, some of the shots were discarded while others were put together so the film would make sense visually.

Bending, Nancy taped several X's on the plywood. As soon as she finished, she helped Lian move the camera for a different angle. Usually this was the job of the dolly grip. But since the budget was tight, everyone had many different roles and jobs.

By the end of the afternoon, one scene had been blocked. Nancy was exhausted. Her hair had dried in a tangle, her clothes felt stiff, and she smelled faintly of dead fish.

When Andrew finally announced, "That's it for today," everybody cheered.

19

"Dinner's on your own tonight," Janie called over the hubbub. "Be here tomorrow morning at eight sharp. Breakfast will be served onboard."

"Whew." George came over. "I'm pooped on the poop deck." Her face was bright red under the brim of her baseball cap.

"Me, too." Nancy leaned against the railing. "I didn't realize how much work was involved in blocking one scene. And shooting takes even longer. What's the rule of thumb we learned?" Nancy thought a second, then answered her own question, "Eight hours of shooting produces six minutes of film."

George groaned. "Does that mean I have to listen to Selena gripe for eight straight hours?"

Nancy laughed. "Maybe she'll lighten up. Ready to go back to the hotel?"

"In a minute. I need to get my fanny pack. It's in the dressing room."

"I'll go with you," Nancy said, following her. "I'd like to see the rest of the ship."

The two girls climbed down the wooden ladder to the waist of the ship. Taking a sharp left, George led Nancy to an open doorway. A short flight of steps descended to a narrow passageway.

Nancy went down the steps, ducking to avoid a lantern that hung from the low ceiling. She saw several closed doors on each side of the dim passageway and one at the far end.

"Daniel told me this is called steerage," George explained. She pointed to the door at the far end. "That's the Great Cabin, where Daniel and Andrew are staying. That opening over there"—she pointed to a half-door in the wall—"leads to the cargo area, where the props are kept."

Bending lower, Nancy stuck her head through the doorway. A wooden ladder led straight into a gray pit. "Why are the props kept all the way down there?"

"They were in one of the cabins in steerage until Selena came," George explained. Opening one of the cabin doors, she gestured inside. "She refused to share this dressing room with anyone. So they kicked Eli and the props out of this cabin and gave it to her."

Brows raised, Nancy stepped inside. The dressing room was tiny. A low wooden shelf jutting from the wall was heaped with clothes. The other wall had two mirrors hanging over a higher narrow shelf piled with makeup, brushes, and bottles. The third wall had pegs to hang clothes. Since there was no porthole, the cabin was stuffy and lighted only by one lantern.

"Can't say I blame her," Nancy murmured.

"Everybody except Selena uses this cabin," George explained, coming in to stand next to Nancy. "So it's a mite crowded."

Nancy turned, bumping into her friend. "Just a mite," she said with a laugh. "Is your fanny pack in all this mess?"

George wrinkled her brow. "Somewhere." She bent to look under the bed, banging Nancy with her elbow.

"I think I'll wait in the hall," Nancy said, and stepped into the passageway.

A loud clunk made her jump. The sound had come from the cargo area. Someone was down below, which was strange, Nancy thought, since no one had passed them.

"George, is there another way to get to the cargo area?" Nancy called into the dressing room.

"Yes. Through a hatch in the bow. But we're not supposed to use it because of the tour groups."

"Hmm." Nancy peered into the pit. She thought about the falling rope. Was someone sneaking around the ship?

"I'm going to look at the props," she told George. And see if there's an intruder, she added to herself as she turned and backed down the ladder.

The cargo area was lighted by one dim lantern. Nancy jumped to the wooden floor, then glanced around. She guessed she was under the quarterdeck. The outside walls of the ship curved like giant ribs. The low ceiling was crossed with beams. Boxes, plastic trash bags, and loose props were stacked randomly as if Eli had moved them in a hurry.

Suddenly another crash made Nancy twirl. Eyes wide, she stared behind her. There was an open doorway that led into the belly of the ship. A shoe box lay in front of the door, its contents of gold doubloons spilled across the floor.

A flash of movement caught Nancy's eye as someone jumped from behind several large boxes and disappeared through the door. Nancy took off after the person, running into a narrow passageway. Instantly, she was enveloped in darkness. She stopped dead. When her eyes adjusted, she saw a dim maze of corridors and entryways winding under the waist of the ship toward the bow.

Nancy knew there was no way she could follow the person without some kind of light. She'd be lost in a second.

Turning, she went back to the cargo hold. The box of spilled doubloons lay in the middle of the floor as if someone had knocked them over in his or her haste to get away.

A shiver tingled up Nancy's spine. Someone *was* sneaking around the ship. But why, and what was the person looking for?

23

3

Ransacked!

Stooping, Nancy picked up one of the gold doubloons and studied it. At first glance, the coin
looked real, but on closer inspection, Nancy
could see the hints of gray pot metal underneath
the gold overlay.

Nancy scooped the fake coins back into the
box. She didn't think someone would want to
steal the obviously fake coins. Perhaps an over-
zealous tourist was hunting for a souvenir, she
thought.

"Nancy!" George called from above. "Are you
coming?"

Hurriedly, Nancy put the lid on the box and
stood up. Before she left for the hotel, she'd have

to tell Andrew that she suspected someone was snooping.

Tucking the box under her arm, she climbed the ladder back to steerage. When George met her at the top, Nancy told her what had happened.

"That's weird. Why would someone be sneaking around the ship?"

"Maybe it's a tourist trying to get a souvenir from the film," Nancy guessed.

"Do you think a tourist would be bold enough to snoop below-decks?" George asked.

"I don't know," Nancy said. "It's puzzling. The intruder had to know his or her way around the ship. I'm going to stash the coins in the dressing room for safekeeping," she added. "Andrew might blow a fuse if one more thing goes wrong. If you see Eli, tell him that's where they are."

Nancy went into the dressing room. It was so crowded with costumes and the cast's and crew's belongings that she had a hard time finding a spot where the box wouldn't get knocked over. Finally, she stashed it under the platform bed.

"Ready?" George asked. They climbed from steerage and onto the quarterdeck, where they found Andrew and Daniel sitting in plastic lawn chairs and looking over the script. Most of the cast and crew had left, and the tourists had disembarked. Other than the squawk of the gulls and the slap of the rigging in the breeze, the ship was quiet and peaceful.

"I'll bet it was punks," Andrew declared when Nancy told him what had happened. "The harbor is crawling with kids who have nothing better to do than trespass. We'll have to see if we can get that hatch door locked."

"Kids?" Daniel snorted. "No self-respecting kid is going to snoop around our cargo hold. I'll bet whoever it was *was* after the doubloons. It could be some tour guide who wants to hand them out as souvenirs. We're quite a tourist attraction, if you hadn't noticed."

Sitting upright, Andrew snapped his fingers. "Hey, that's not a bad idea. When it comes time to promote the film, we can use doubloons in the ads."

"Well, I just wanted to let you know." Nancy could tell the twins weren't too worried. "I put the box of doubloons in the women's dressing room for safekeeping."

"Thanks," Andrew said, then continued discussing with his brother ways to promote the film.

"They didn't seem concerned," George said as they left the quarterdeck.

"That's for sure. And right now, I'm too sticky and tired to think about the snooper, either." Nancy brushed a limp strand of hair off her forehead. "Just lead me to the hotel and point me to the shower!"

"I'll have two of everything," George declared an hour later as she read the hotel menu. "I'm as hungry as, well, as a pirate!"

Nancy laughed. "Me, too. And everything looks good. Maryland's famous for its crab cakes, so I think that's what I'm going to order."

Both girls had showered and changed into lightweight slacks and short-sleeved shirts. Nancy had brought a jacket and George a sweater since they hoped to explore the Inner Harbor after dinner.

"The grilled salmon sounds heavenly," George said as she studied her menu. "With a shrimp cocktail appetizer."

"Shrimp sounds good to me, too." Closing her menu, Nancy glanced around. She noticed the restaurant had a nautical theme. Framed photographs of the harbor area before it had been renovated and famous sailing ships dotted the walls.

The dining room was full, Nancy noticed, but she didn't see anyone from the cast and crew. "I guess no one else is staying at the hotel except Selena," she said to George. "And she probably orders room service."

"*Orders* is right," George said with a chuckle.

"You'll be just as haughty when you're a famous actress," Nancy teased.

"A famous actress?" someone said.

Nancy glanced up. Their waiter stood by her elbow, looking expectantly at George. He was cute, with sandy blond hair. He looked to be about their age, Nancy guessed, though she knew he had to be at least twenty-one to work in the hotel restaurant.

"Can I get your autograph?" the waiter asked George, a hint of laughter in his sky-blue eyes.

George giggled. "Sure. Though unless you're a fan of educational TV, I doubt you'll ever catch my big debut."

The waiter snapped his fingers. *"Robbers of the High Seas,* right?"

George stared at him in surprise. "Right. How'd you guess?"

He smiled and shrugged. Nancy liked his open, friendly grin. "When Selena Ramirez checked in, everybody started talking about the film. Plus, I took filmmaking courses in college, so I was naturally curious. But hey"—his expression turned serious—"I'm here to take your order. You guys look starved."

After they ordered and he left, George leaned across the table. "He's cute."

"Oh, really?" Nancy replied as if she hadn't noticed.

Minutes later, when he brought their salads and rolls, he introduced himself. "I'm Scott Harlow," he said. "I'm waiting tables to earn money for graduate school."

Nancy and George introduced themselves, then George asked, "Have you lived in Baltimore a long time?"

"All my life. So if you need a tour guide, I'm at your service." He gave a mock bow. Then, leaning closer, he added, "So, is Selena Ramirez as gorgeous in person as she is in her films? Not that *I'm* a fan of hers." He gestured to another waiter. "John is dying to meet her."

"Once he does, he'll run for his life," George said under her breath. Nancy burst out laughing. When Scott gave her a puzzled look, she said, "Selena is temperamental. I doubt she'd give John the time of day. But maybe we can get him an autograph for you."

"Great!" Scott beamed. "Anything else I can get you?" When they both said no, he went over to another table.

"I'll bet he wants the autograph for himself," George whispered.

"Maybe not. It's funny, though—working with Selena, I forget she's a fairly well-known actress."

"That's because you're too busy trying to forget her," George said.

For the next fifteen minutes, the two ate ravenously. When Nancy was finished with her salad, she pulled a brochure from her fanny pack. George was buttering a hot roll.

"What should we see tonight?" Nancy asked. "The aquarium and science center will probably be closed by the time we finish dinner."

Just then Scott came up, a round tray balanced on one hand. "I overheard you talking about what to do. May I suggest a nighttime cruise," he said, taking a dinner plate off the tray. The tray tipped, and Nancy gasped as the dishes slid sideways heading right for her lap.

"Whoa!" Just in time, Scott leveled the tray. "Sorry." He glanced nervously back at the closed door of the kitchen as if worried someone had seen him. "I wasn't paying attention," he explained, giving Nancy an apologetic grin.

"One order of salmon," he said, setting George's plate in front of her. It hit her drink glass with a clink. When the glass threatened to tip, George grabbed it, righting it just in time.

"Crab cakes, right?" He came around to Nancy's side.

"Yes." She grabbed onto her own glass. "A night cruise sounds cool."

"Oh, it is cool," Scott agreed enthusiastically. "The city lights reflecting in the harbor water are spectacular."

George speared a bite of salmon. "Sounds good to me. When does the boat leave?"

"Nine o'clock. The *Baltimore Lady* is docked right in front of the hotel, so you'll have plenty of time. Is there anything else I can get you?"

"No thanks," Nancy said.

"I'll be back in a bit to make sure everything's okay."

When he bustled off, George giggled. "A little overeager, don't you think?"

"Maybe he gets a kickback from any tourist he steers to the cruise." Nancy took a bite of the crab cake. "Umm. Heavenly."

Half an hour later, they finished eating, and Scott brought them their check. "I get off in fifteen minutes," he told them. "Maybe I'll join you on the tour boat."

"That would be fun," Nancy said, meaning it. In between waiting on customers, he'd told them a lot of interesting facts about Baltimore.

After they paid their check, Nancy and George went into the lobby and out the front doors. The harbor and all its attractions were right across the street. Nancy could see the *Baltimore Lady* from the front of the hotel.

Fifteen minutes later, Nancy and George had bought tickets and were boarding the cruise ship. It was crowded with groups and couples.

"I don't see Scott," Nancy said, glancing around at the other passengers.

"Do I detect disappointment?" George teased as they made their way to an upper deck. Nancy leaned over the railing. The water of the harbor shimmered like black glass. As Scott had promised, the lights of the buildings were reflected clearly in it.

"Nancy! George!" someone called a few minutes later. Nancy turned to see Scott weaving through the crowd. He'd taken off his waiter's jacket and had put on a crewneck sweater. "Glad I made it."

"Is the dinner shift already over?" Nancy asked.

Scott grimaced. "I've been waiting tables since lunch. I only filled in tonight because one of the waitresses was sick. The big dinner rush was over, so the manager let me leave early."

"Good. You can be our unofficial tour guide," George said. A loud blast from the ship's horn made Nancy turn back around. Slowly, the *Baltimore Lady* pulled away from the wharf.

For the next half hour, Scott, Nancy, and George enjoyed the cruise. A band played on the enclosed middle deck. A bar served soft drinks on the open top deck. The three spent most of their time hanging over the railing, watching the sights and discussing filmmaking and pirates.

When they returned to the wharf area, Scott said goodnight. "I've got to work dinner shift tomorrow, so maybe I'll see you then."

After Nancy and George said goodbye, they

headed for the elevator. Their room was on the third floor.

Nancy was exhausted. "I thought the sea air was supposed to be invigorating," she said, stifling a yawn.

"That must be an old pirate's tale," George said.

When they reached their room, the girls quickly changed into their pajamas and crawled into bed. They were both asleep by ten.

Loud voices woke Nancy up. She blinked her eyes, trying to figure out where the voices were coming from. Sitting up, she oriented herself to the dark hotel room.

She glanced toward the door. Several people were chattering in the hall. Nancy checked the digital clock on the table between the two beds. Two in the morning. Must be late-night partygoers, she decided.

Lying back down, she pulled the covers to her chin and shut her eyes. Several people hurried down the hall, their feet thumping on the carpet. Then the voices grew louder.

Holding her breath, Nancy listened closely. The voices sounded worried and urgent. Then Nancy heard the unmistakable squawk of a walkie-talkie.

Her eyes snapped open. Those were definitely

not late-night partiers. Climbing from bed, she tiptoed to the door and listened.

"Lab techs will be right here," someone was saying. "Officer Kelsey, you need to get statements from everyone on the hall."

"Can't this wait until morning?" a shrill voice protested. "I can't have you waking our guests in the middle of the night."

Like your shouting isn't going to wake us up first, Nancy thought.

"No, it can't wait," the first voice answered firmly. "The sooner we find our burglar, the sooner we can return the stolen goods to your guests."

Burglar! Nancy's eyes widened.

"Nancy!" George hissed from her bed. "What's going on?"

"Sounds like some of the rooms on our hall were burglarized," Nancy explained, flicking on the bathroom light. "The police are out there. I'm getting dressed to go see what's going on."

"Wait for me!" George exclaimed as she leaped out of bed.

Nancy pulled on a shirt and jeans, then opened the door and went into the hall. The bright lights momentarily blinded her, and she stood for a second to get her bearings.

Several police officers were standing in the hall. Nancy counted three doors wide open with yellow crime tape stretched across each door. In front of one door, a tall man in a sport coat was talking to the hotel concierge, who was wringing his hands worriedly.

"Find your guests other rooms for the night," the man was saying. "But first, they'll need to inventory their things and tell us exactly what was taken. As soon as the lab techs are finished, they can have their other suitcases."

The concierge threw up his hands in dismay. "This has never before happened at the Harborside," he said. "Our guests will not be pleased."

The concierge was turning to go when he caught sight of Nancy. "See? You have awakened a guest already!"

He hurried over to Nancy. "Miss, I apologize for the inconvenience. Please, we will get you a room on another hall."

"No, that's okay, really," Nancy said.

"We're used to robbery and mayhem," George added as she came out of the room to stand beside Nancy. She'd hurriedly dressed, too, slipping on a sweatshirt and jeans.

The concierge gave them a puzzled look, then bustled to intercept another guest. Walking down the hall, Nancy peered into the first taped-off room. A suitcase had been emptied onto the floor. Pillows, clothes, and shoes were strewn around.

"What a mess," George said. "The robbers must have been in a hurry."

"They were probably hunting for cash and jewelry," Nancy told George. "Though they missed some," she added, catching sight of something gold and glittery on the bed. When she looked closer, she realized with a jolt what it was—a gold doubloon, exactly like the ones from the ship!

4

Suspicion Onboard

What was a gold doubloon doing in the hotel room? Nancy wondered. Did it belong to the guests in that room? Had the thieves dropped it?

"Excuse me."

Startled, Nancy whirled, and found herself face-to-face with the tall man in the sport coat.

"I'm Detective Jackson Weller from the Robbery Unit of the Baltimore Police Department," he said to Nancy and George. "What room are you ladies staying in?" he asked as he took a pad and pen from his coat pocket.

"Room thirty-four," Nancy said. "How many rooms were burglarized?"

"Three. Did either of you hear anything unusual?"

George and Nancy shook their heads. "We were sound asleep until voices woke us," Nancy added.

"What time did you go to your room?"

"About ten," George replied. "We took the nine o'clock cruise on the *Baltimore Lady*. It was over about nine forty-five. It took us about fifteen minutes to get back to the room. Yup. Ten." George nodded emphatically. "And we didn't see anyone else in the hall or hear any strange noises. Right, Nancy?"

"Right," Nancy said.

Detective Weller cocked one brow. "You two seem awfully sure of your every movement," he said suspiciously.

Nancy suppressed a grin. "That's because I'm a detective. George has helped me with a lot of cases, so we know the drill." She held out her hand. "Nancy Drew from River Heights. This is my friend, George Fayne."

Ignoring Nancy's hand, Weller wrote down their names, muttering, "Must be a detective convention at the hotel or something."

Nancy could tell he wasn't convinced they were telling the truth. Her gaze flicked to the gold doubloon on the bed. Since it was in plain sight, the police must have noticed it. Sooner or later, they were sure to trace it to the *Swift Adventure*, she concluded.

"You heard or saw nothing unusual," Weller persisted.

"No," Nancy told him. "We were tired. When we came up in the elevator to our floor, there was no one else around. So, what was stolen?" she asked curiously.

"We can't give out that kind of information." Putting his hand firmly on her elbow, he steered her toward the door. "Thank you very much, Ms. Drew and Ms. Fayne. If you think of anything else, please call me at this number." He handed Nancy a card, then headed toward the concierge, who was talking to a couple wearing bathrobes.

"He's not very friendly," George commented when they went into their rooms. "And he sure looked at us suspiciously."

"I can't blame him," Nancy said. "This isn't River Heights where almost everyone knows I'm a detective. Besides, a good investigator suspects everybody."

"Well, we're not guilty, that's for sure." George fell onto her bed. "We were in here all night snoring happily."

"Right," Nancy replied as she stopped at the end of her bed to take off her jeans. "George, did you notice the gold coin on the bed in the room that was burglarized?"

"A coin?" George mumbled, her head buried in her pillow.

"Yes. Just like the doubloons we're using for props in the movie."

George's head popped up. "You're kidding."

"No." Sitting on the bed, Nancy pulled off her shirt. "I wouldn't have thought much about it except I keep remembering the mysterious person in the cargo area."

"Do you think there's a connection?" George asked.

"Could be." Nancy yawned sleepily as she crawled under the covers.

"Tomorrow we need to tell Daniel and Andrew what happened," she continued. "Sooner or later Detective Weller will figure out where the coin came from." She sighed. "I just hope it's later. Until then, I want to do a little investigating myself. Let's hope that doubloon had *nothing* to do with the robbery."

On Tuesday morning Nancy and George hurried to the *Swift Adventure*. Most of the cast and crew were onboard, eating and talking. Janie had laid out a buffet breakfast of doughnuts, bagels, fruit, and juice on a makeshift table on the quarterdeck.

"Looks delicious," George said as she made a beeline for a box of doughnuts.

"Save me a glazed," Nancy called. She needed to talk to Andrew and Daniel as soon as possible.

The twins were standing by the stern railing,

talking to a man in a dress shirt and tie. "Five hundred dollars?" Nancy heard Andrew exclaim. "For a couple of sticks of wood!"

When Nancy drew closer, she saw that they were standing next to the broken railing where Harold had fallen overboard.

"Not just sticks of wood, Mr. Wagner," the man explained. "They have to be carefully crafted to match the existing rail."

"Look, just give me a knife and a chunk of wood and I'll whittle one myself," Andrew retorted. He ran his fingers through his hair, obviously exasperated. And tired, Nancy thought, noting the dark circles under his eyes.

The man gave him an annoyed look. "I can tell you don't value historical accuracy."

Daniel chuckled. He wore his usual baggy shorts and shirt. A bright red bandanna was tied around his head. "That's what I've been telling him all week, Mr. Perry. He keeps buying props from toy stores and discount places."

Perry. Nancy remembered the name. He was the man from the historical society whom Janie had dealt with when she'd requested permission to use the ship for the film.

"I will send you the estimate tomorrow," Mr. Perry continued. "It will probably take a week for the job to get done. Until then, the carpenters will make a temporary railing. For safety's sake, keep this area off-limits. When the new railing is

41

finished, I will expect you to pay the bill promptly. Good day."

He turned so quickly that he almost bumped into Nancy. With a terse "Excuse me," he left.

Andrew's scowling gaze shifted to Nancy. "Good morning, assistant director."

"Why was he in such a huff?" Nancy asked.

Daniel laughed. "It must have been Andrew's earlier comment about wormy old wood."

"I hope you brought me some good news," Andrew said. "So far, this film has been jinxed."

Nancy wrinkled her nose. "Um, I'm afraid my news—"

Just then she saw Detective Weller climb the ladder to the quarterdeck. Had he traced the doubloon to the *Swift Adventure* already? Nancy wondered.

"—is not good. I was hoping to tell you before the police did."

"The police!" Andrew and Daniel said in unison.

"The man coming onboard is with the Baltimore police department," Nancy explained.

The twins turned to see to whom she was referring. "What's he doing here?" Daniel asked in a low voice.

Nancy opened her mouth to give them a brief explanation, but Weller was already striding across the deck, his attention focused on Nancy.

"Why, if it isn't Ms. Drew." Pulling the pad from his pocket, he flipped back the pages, then read, "River Heights. Heard nothing unusual."

Nancy smiled politely. "That's me."

"What's going on?" Andrew demanded.

Weller turned his intense gaze on him. "And you are?"

Andrew and Daniel introduced themselves, then Andrew repeated his question. Detective Weller explained about the burglary and finding the gold doubloon.

"So what?" Andrew propped his hands on his hips. "Why do you think it came from here?"

"We got an anonymous tip," Weller explained.

An anonymous tip! "What did the caller say?" Nancy asked.

"Someone phoned 911 early this morning," Weller explained. "They told the operator that the gold doubloon found in the burglarized room came from this ship."

"Wait a minute," Nancy said to Weller. "Don't you think that's suspicious? If the coin didn't belong to the guests, then the burglar must have left it, which meant he or she called in the tip."

"Perhaps." Weller glanced around the ship as if expecting to spot the robber in the crowd.

"I'm very confused here," Daniel said. "Will someone explain to me what's going on?"

Nancy filled in Daniel and Andrew about the

43

last night's burglaries and the gold doubloon. Then she turned back to Detective Weller. "Was there a coin in every room that was burglarized?"

"Good deduction, Ms. Drew." He held out a piece of paper. "I have a search warrant. I'd appreciate it if one of you would show me where the doubloons are kept and give me a list of people who have access to them."

"Officer, uh, Mr., uh, whoever you are," Andrew sputtered. "We have a film to shoot. Unless you are accusing us of—"

"I'll take him," Nancy cut in before Andrew made Weller angry. "The box of coins is in one of the cabins that's being used as a dressing room," she explained as she led the detective down the ladder to the main deck.

A police officer was standing at the top of the gangplank. Nancy glanced at her watch. The tour groups started in half an hour. She wondered if the police were going to keep them from coming onto the ship.

"Ms. Drew." Detective Weller stopped Nancy before they went down the steps into steerage. "Don't you think it's more than a coincidence that you, a person who obviously knows about the coins, are also a guest on the floor that was robbed?"

Cocking one brow, Nancy gave him a cool look. Actually, it was just the kind of question she would have asked. "Yes," she replied honestly.

"And if you doubt my innocence, I suggest you call Chief McGinnis of the River Heights Police Department."

Weller wrote the name on his pad. "I think I'll do just that."

Nancy made her way through the dark passageway to the dressing room. The box of doubloons was still stashed under the bed.

Nancy considered telling Weller how she'd almost caught someone trying to take them, then stopped herself. If the detective thought she was involved in the burglaries, he would think she'd made up the story to cast suspicion on someone else.

It looked more and more as if the mysterious person in the cargo hold had indeed been after the doubloons, Nancy thought. She decided to do some investigating as soon as she had the chance to look around on her own.

"This room isn't kept locked?" Weller asked.

"No. Only cast and crew are allowed down here, though," Nancy said.

Weller exhaled loudly. "Then we'll have to interview everyone."

Squatting, he opened the box and took out one of the coins. "Identical to the one on the bed. Who purchased them for the film?"

"I believe Daniel Wagner did. Eli Wakefield is in charge of props, so he might be able to tell you where they came from."

"Thank you." He followed Nancy to the ship's waist, then excused himself to go to his police car. Nancy climbed the steps to the quarterdeck. George, Janie, Selena, Andrew, Daniel, and several other cast and crew members were huddled in a circle, talking.

Nancy heard Karl Kidd's loud voice bellow, "It was pirates, all right. Who else would be brazen enough to rob landlubbers in a posh hotel?"

"Sounds like you want to invite these cunning cutthroats to join the cast," Daniel joked.

"Did Weller come to his senses and decide we had nothing to do with the robbery?" Andrew asked when Nancy came over.

She grimaced. "Not exactly. In fact, he's probably requesting more officers so he can interview everybody."

Andrew threw his hands up in the air. "That's great. More delays. Just what I need on top of a five-hundred-dollar repair bill."

"Maybe this ship is haunted by the ghost of Blackbeard," Janie said in a spooky-sounding voice. "He's telling us he doesn't want this film made."

Everyone laughed, except Andrew, who rapped on his clipboard. "Attention. We're doing a dress rehearsal of scene three in fifteen minutes. Daniel, Selena, and George, we need—"

While Andrew was giving instructions, Nancy

slipped away. She wanted to do her investigating before Weller came back.

Quickly, she headed down the steps into steerage, then down the ladder into the cargo area. This time she took a flashlight. If someone had stolen the doubloons, he or she might have left a clue. If so, Nancy was determined to find it before the police swarmed over the ship.

When she reached the cargo area, she carefully searched behind boxes and bags but found nothing unusual. Flicking on the flashlight, she went into the passageway that led from the cargo area into the belly of the ship.

Nancy shivered. It was dark, damp, and musty. After taking ten cautious steps, she beamed the light around, trying to get her bearings.

She was in the top cargo where the pumps were located. Passing a section of the huge, round mainmast, she stopped and peered into a dark hole that led to the ship's hold. Below that was the bilge, the lowest part of the ship's hull.

Nancy shone the light into the hold. She didn't think the person fleeing from the cargo area would have gone below since he or she would have been trapped. Her guess was the person ran for the hatch in the ship's bow.

She made her way along another passage until she came to a ladder in a room filled with wooden barrels and boxes. Raising the flashlight's beam, she found the rectangular outline of the bow hatch. When she climbed the ladder, she was able to push up one of the doors. Despite what Andrew had said the day before, no one had come down and locked it.

Nancy was climbing down the ladder when a movement behind a barrel made her freeze. Heart thumping, she aimed the light at the barrel, illuminating a scrap of light-colored fabric.

Nancy stifled a gasp. Someone *was* hiding behind the barrel!

5

A Crew of Thieves

Nancy's first thought was to flee up the ladder onto the main deck. But she checked herself. She had to find out who was hiding in the hold. The person could be the key to the burglaries.

"Who's there?" she called in a firm voice. "Come out with your hands in front of you before I call the police."

"Take it easy," a deep voice said. A second later a man stepped from behind the barrel, his arms held away from his sides. "I'm unarmed."

Frowning, Nancy kept the light directed on the man's face. He blinked, then turned his head away. He was dressed casually in a white, short-sleeve shirt and jeans. His dark hair was wavy, his skin tan. Nancy figured he was in his mid-twenties. An expensive-looking camera hung from a strap around his neck.

"Who are you and what are you doing here?" she demanded.

"I'm Joseph Mascelli, a reporter for the *Baltimore City Express*," the man explained. "My press card is clipped to my shirt pocket."

Nancy lowered the beam to the photo on the card, which matched the man's face. "What are you doing down here?"

"Uh," Mascelli began. "I'm trying to get a story on the film."

Nancy raised one brow. "Good try, but I don't buy it. You'd be on deck, interviewing Selena Ramirez."

"I took the wrong ladder?" Mascelli quipped.

"No, and if you don't come up with the right answer, I'm going to scream, alerting the cops who are boarding right about now. You'll be charged with trespassing, since this area is closed off to the public."

"In that case, I guess I have no choice." Still squinting, Mascelli turned his head toward her. "Do you mind shining that thing somewhere else?"

Nancy tapped her foot. "I'm waiting."

"All right." Mascelli dropped his arms by his sides. "I got an anonymous tip about the burglary at the Harborside Hotel. Something about pirates and gold doubloons. I figured it had to be connected with the film."

Another anonymous tip! Nancy bit her lip, trying to figure out who was so eager to throw suspicion on the movie's cast and crew. When she'd first been alerted to someone behind the barrel, she thought she might have caught her mysterious snooper. Obviously, Mascelli wasn't him—or her.

"Now, how about telling me who *you* are?" Mascelli asked.

"The film's assistant director," Nancy said. "And I suggest if you have any other questions, you ask for an interview instead of sneaking around the ship."

"Good idea." He pulled a small tape recorder from his pocket and clicked it on. "So tell me. Ms., uh . . ."

"Drew."

"Drew. Are the rumors true? Were gold doubloons left in the burglarized rooms? Are pirates involved in the thefts at the Harborside Hotel?"

Nancy smiled in mock-innocence. "No comment. Now, may I escort you off the ship?"

With a snort of annoyance, Mascelli switched the recorder off. "You really should talk to me. I'll get my story one way or another."

"You can ask the director of the film, Andrew Wagner, for an interview," she suggested.

Nancy heard the thudding of hard-soled shoes

51

on the deck above. Stepping away from the ladder, she gestured to the hatch. "You first."

Scowling, Mascelli went up the ladder, pushing open both hatch doors. Bright sunshine poured into the hold, and when Nancy climbed out, she had to shade her eyes.

Two uniformed officers had boarded with Detective Weller. The three men stood talking on the waist, unaware that Nancy or Mascelli had just ascended from the hold.

"No one is to leave the ship until everyone has been interviewed," Weller said, loudly enough for Nancy to hear. "We need to check out everyone's alibis, noting where they were between the hours of midnight and one in the morning. My hunch is someone in the cast or crew is our thief. And I want to catch that person *now*."

Raising his camera to his eye, Mascelli snapped several pictures without the officers knowing. Then, turning to face Nancy, he gave her a cocky grin. "Well, Ms. Drew, it looks as if I got my big scoop after all." Raising one arm, he made an arc in the air. "'Pirates Raid the Inner Harbor.' I think it'll make a great headline."

"Only it won't be true," Nancy said quickly, though she wasn't sure herself.

Mascelli jerked his thumb toward the police officers. "It is according to the 'quote' I just got from them," he said. With a triumphant grin, he strode across the waist, waving cheerfully to the startled police officers.

"Who was that?" Weller said, coming over to Nancy.

"Joseph Mascelli, ace reporter," she muttered.

Weller shook his head. "I thought I recognized him. That means we'd better work fast. I don't want tomorrow's news sending our thief into hiding."

Rejoining the other officers, he led them up to the quarterdeck. Nancy pushed her hair behind her ears. Her investigating had turned up something all right. Too bad it wasn't going to help solve the case.

"Selena, you're a pirate, not a beauty queen," Andrew told the star during dress rehearsal two hours later. The officers had spent the morning interviewing everyone involved with the film. When they'd left, Nancy had asked Detective Weller if he'd discovered anything, but he'd tersely replied, "No comment."

"You're supposed to look messy, Selena," Andrew continued. "For three weeks you've been on board a ship with no shower, wearing the same clothes."

Selena wrinkled her nose. She and George were standing at the ship's wheel, pretending to be navigating through a storm. Both wore their costumes.

Nancy thought George looked great. She wore a red scarf tied around her head and knotted in the back, a loose linen shirt, and baggy breeches held up by a sash around her waist. A pistol and dagger were tucked into the sash.

"That's gross!" Selena exclaimed with a toss of her long ponytail. "I don't care what the real Mary Read was like. I refuse to look like an old man and smell like an old fish."

Nancy laughed along with the rest of the cast and crew. After several hours of police interviews, everyone needed a chuckle.

All morning Andrew had groused about the delay. Then Detective Weller had taken the director into the Great Cabin for an interview. Fifteen minutes later, Andrew had stormed out. Nancy was dying to ask what had made him so angry, but she hadn't been able to get him alone.

"You know, Andrew," Janie said, striding up to Selena, "it can't hurt to have her looking slightly gorgeous." She pulled out the rawhide tie from Selena's ponytail and fluffed the actress's hair so the wind caught it.

Selena frowned pensively as she gazed out to sea. The effect was perfect. Nancy thought she looked exotic and slightly dangerous.

Janie stepped back and made a rectangle with her fingers. "Picture this shot on a publicity poster."

"You're right, Janie," Andrew said with a

smile. "I guess that's why I hired you for my production manager."

"*And* because I'm working for free," Janie added saucily.

Everybody laughed—everybody except George, Nancy noticed. George looked slightly disgruntled. Not that Nancy blamed her. For the last hour, Selena had purposefully upstaged her, reciting her lines with such Shakespearian passion that Daniel had finally yelled, "You're a ruthless pirate, Selena. Not Juliet."

Going up to her friend, Nancy whispered, "Hang in there, George. You're doing great."

"All right, let's try that again," Andrew said. "Take it from the line where Anne Bonny says, 'All hands aloft!'"

"Mr. Wagner!" a loud voice interrupted. Nancy turned to see a small group of people charging across the deck. She glanced at Andrew. One more delay and he might explode.

But the director had hopped off his stool and was approaching the woman in front with his hand outstretched. "Ms. Weems? I'm delighted you're here."

Delighted? Nancy raised her brows. Behind Ms. Weems, a man carried a heavy camera on his shoulder, a WCBN news logo on his shirt.

"A TV station?" she heard Daniel boom behind her. Scowling, Daniel strode across the deck to join his brother. From the expression on his face, Nancy figured he had no idea what his twin was up to.

"More publicity?" George asked, coming up beside Nancy. "After the police were here all morning, we're already going to be in the headlines."

"Looks like it," Nancy agreed. "Only Ms. Weems was definitely invited."

Just then Selena sashayed past. "Ooh, a camera. That's my cue to make a grand entrance."

"I'd like to give her an entrance—down a long plank into the ocean," George growled when Selena was out of earshot.

Nancy burst out laughing. "Don't tell me my friend George Fayne is jealous."

"Not jealous—frustrated." George pulled off her scarf and wiped her sweaty brow. "I'm really trying to do a good job. I've read so much about pirates, I dream about them. But Selena's making every scene sound like something from a bad romance."

"Nancy! George! I want you to meet Maria Weems of WCBN-TV. We're going to be featured on the network's 'What's Happening' segment tomorrow night."

Andrew walked around, introducing the rest of the cast. "Ms. Weems is going to be interviewing and taping us this afternoon," he explained.

George leaned closer and whispered to Nancy, "Gee, I can't imagine why. Do you think they would have been the least bit interested in us if the Harborside hadn't been robbed?"

"Just what I was thinking," Nancy said.

"Oh, the production has been cursed from the beginning," Nancy heard someone say behind her. She twisted around to see Selena leaning against the ship's wheel, her hair artfully arranged around her shoulders. The cameraman was taping her while a younger man asked questions.

"Not that I believe the crew when they suggest the ghost of Blackbeard is involved." Cocking her head, Selena smiled winningly at the camera. "You'll have to ask Karl Kidd about that. He's the actor portraying the ruthless villain."

"That's me!" Karl boomed as he strode across the deck. "Ask me anything you want about pirates. I'm a walking encyclopedia."

The cameraman turned toward him, and Selena frowned. She waltzed over to Karl, linked arms with him, and beamed at the lens.

"That woman has more moves than a hula dancer," George said with a chuckle. "I think she'd do anything for attention."

"Anything?" Nancy repeated.

George's eyes widened as if she realized what Nancy was getting at. "No . . . you can't possibly think—"

"That Selena robbed the rooms last night?" Nancy shook her head. "No, but I do believe she's taking full advantage of it. Since she's staying at the hotel, she could have easily heard about the burglaries. What if she sneaked down and saw the doubloons?"

"And made the anonymous tip." George finished Nancy's thought.

"Tips," Nancy clarified. She told George about finding Mascelli in the ship. "He said someone called the newspaper this morning as well."

"Wow. We'll definitely be front-page news," George said. "If Selena was the tipster, she'd get exactly what she craves—publicity."

"Right." Nancy's gaze shifted to Andrew, who was escorting Maria Weems around the quarter-deck as if she were a queen.

He's just as crazy about publicity as Selena is, Nancy thought. She knew he was worried continually about money. Could he be behind the thefts?

It was a definite possibility, Nancy decided. He could have burglarized the rooms for much-needed cash, then cleverly left the doubloons, hoping the police would trace them to the film. Instant cash, instant publicity—not bad for one night's work.

6

A Daring Heist

"We're never going to get this scene shot if these TV people hang around," Daniel grumbled as he came over, interrupting Nancy's thoughts. In his costume as Calico Jack Rackham, he looked just as authentic as George. He wore a tricornered hat, a red bandanna around his neck, loose green pants with a yellow sash, and a frayed naval uniform jacket. Around his chest he had a gunbelt with a pistol tucked into it.

"And it doesn't look as if Andrew cares," George said, sounding puzzled.

"That *is* odd," Nancy agreed.

Daniel grunted. Untying the bandanna, he squirted water on it from a bottle he was carrying. "Newspeople are like hawks," he said, wiping his neck and cheeks with the wet cloth. "Circling for the big kill."

"You had nothing to do with setting up the interviews?" Nancy asked.

"No way. They'll just distract the crew, misquote the cast, and get their facts wrong."

A sharp voice drew Nancy's attention away from Daniel. Janie was facing Andrew, poking him in the chest with one finger, an angry expression on her face. Because they were on the other side of the quarterdeck, Nancy couldn't hear what Janie was saying.

"What's that all about?" George asked.

Daniel shook his head. "Andrew must have ordered her around one too many times."

"Everybody's tense," Nancy said, though she couldn't help but wonder what had caused Janie to blow up. The production manager worked hard to stay professional. With all the strange things going on, Nancy decided she'd better have a talk with Janie.

"We'll be back late," George told Nancy as she checked her hair in the hotel room mirror one more time.

"What are you and Daniel going to do after dinner?" Nancy asked, zipping up her denim skirt.

George turned to face her. "We're going to Fort McHenry, then we'll walk back along the wharf. It's a beautiful night, and we need some-place quiet to practice our lines. So, how do I look?"

Nancy grinned. As always, her friend was dressed casually in jeans, but she'd added dangling earrings, sandals, and a colorful vest. "You look like Daniel's fashion sense rubbed off on you."

George grinned, obviously pleased with Nancy's response. "What are you and Janie going to do?" she asked as she snapped her fanny pack around her waist.

"I'm treating her to dinner at the hotel," Nancy said. "She needs a little TLC after today."

"Good idea," George said, waving goodbye as she left.

Fifteen minutes later Nancy and Janie were seated in the hotel restaurant at a table overlooking the Inner Harbor. Janie had put on a one-piece red dress. Her straight brown hair was smoothed behind her ears and pinned with a butterfly barrette.

"You look great tonight," Nancy commented as she opened her menu.

Janie shrugged. "Not that anybody will notice."

"Oh? Were you hoping someone in particular would notice?" Nancy teased lightly.

"No. It's just that hanging around Selena, I feel invisible. Guys look right through me."

"Hey, Nancy and . . . ?" Scott came up, his order pad in hand.

Nancy smiled. "This is Janie Simms, the production manager on the film. George and one of the other actors are out sightseeing and practicing lines."

Scott's eyes lit up. "Nice to meet you, Janie. As far as I'm concerned, being a production manager is the best. So much control. So much responsibility."

"So much grief," Janie added with a sigh. "If the crew doesn't like the food, they complain to me. If the cast doesn't like the schedule, they complain to me. If the director needs a scapegoat . . ." Her voice trailed off.

"Sounds like a fun job," Scott joked.

"Scott's interested in filmmaking," Nancy said.

"Why don't you come watch tomorrow?" Janie suggested. "The *Good Morning Baltimore* show is going to be taping it for one of their programs."

"Count me in," Scott said. "You guys are famous, you know. Today you were splashed all over the front page of every newspaper. Pretty exciting, huh?" He glanced back and forth at Nancy and Janie as he spoke, then said in a low voice, "The word around the hotel is that the thief had a master key card to break into the guests' rooms."

Nancy pricked up her ears. She'd never thought about pumping Scott about the thefts.

Now she realized what a perfect source he would be.

"Then the thief had to have a link with the hotel," Nancy guessed.

Scott pointed his pad at her and said, "That's what the police think. Yesterday afternoon they interrogated everybody from laundry workers to waitpersons."

"So we weren't the only ones harassed," Janie said with a snort.

Nancy stared at her menu, her thoughts on Scott's news. Had the police uncovered any new evidence about the burglaries? she wondered.

After the two gave Scott their dinner orders, Nancy asked Janie, "What do you think about Detective Weller's accusation that one of the cast or crew members is the thief?"

"I think it's baloney," Janie stated firmly. "I know everybody working on the film. We've either worked together before, or I went to school with them."

"Even Karl Kidd?" Nancy asked.

"We worked on a Shakespeare production together. Karl's a little wacky, but he's no thief."

"Mind if I ask what you and Andrew were arguing about this afternoon?"

With a sigh, Janie slumped back in her seat. "The same thing we always argue about—money. Yesterday Andrew worried over every delay. Then today he invites the TV crew onboard. We lost several hours of filming. Tomorrow he's got the morning show coming. I reminded him that we can't afford any more delays. He basically told me to shut up."

Nancy listened carefully, taking it all in. It sounded as though her hunch about Andrew was right. It would explain why he had done such an about-face on the money issue.

"Your salad has arrived," Scott announced. With a dramatic swoop of his arm, he set Nancy's plate on the table, knocking her purse onto the floor.

"Oops. Sorry," he apologized, stooping to pick it up.

Nancy laughed. "When Scott visits tomorrow, Janie, you'd better keep a close eye on him. We don't need another person falling overboard!"

When they had finished dinner, Nancy suggested catching the concert at Pier Six.

"Thanks, but I'd better head back to my room," Janie said. Janie and several of the other crew members were staying at a smaller, budget hotel several blocks away.

"It's been a lo-o-ng day." Dropping her napkin on the table, Janie stood up. "Thanks so much for dinner. I needed a break."

"Glad I could treat you. See you tomorrow." Nancy watched her friend leave, then leaned back and waited for the check. Janie's information about Andrew was certainly incriminating. She wondered if Detective Weller had uncovered information about the film's money problems yet.

"A big tip for your thoughts," Scott said, coming up beside her. Nancy glanced up. He had such a friendly smile on his face that she couldn't help smiling back.

"Actually, I was thinking I should give you a big tip for *your* thoughts," Nancy said. "What else are the hotel employees saying about the thefts?"

"They're all saying 'I didn't do it!' " he declared in a mock-indignant voice, then laughed. "Really, I don't know anything more. But if I hear anything else, I'll let you know."

"Thanks. And see you tomorrow," Nancy added as he handed her the check.

After paying the bill, Nancy started for her room. But when she reached the elevator, she realized she was too keyed up to sleep. Besides, it was only nine o'clock. Maybe an ice cream cone and a walk would help her relax.

She went into Harborplace, and for an hour browsed in a few of the boutiques and specialty stores housed in the two-story glass pavilion. On the way out, she bought a cone at one of the food booths, then went down to the wharf and sat on a brick wall near where a mariachi band was playing.

A crowd had gathered. Some children danced to the lively music, swinging each other square-dance style, while their parents clapped. Nancy was enjoying the catchy rhythm when she saw Janie Simms striding purposefully along the wharf.

Her hotel is in the opposite direction, Nancy thought, wondering where Janie was going in such a hurry. Any other time, she wouldn't have been so curious. But Janie had said she was going back to the hotel.

A cold drip plopped on her wrist. Nancy quickly licked the ice cream dribbling down the sides of the cone. Standing, she started after Janie, stopping abruptly when she saw Karl Kidd.

The big actor was walking in the same direction as Janie and was about twenty-five feet behind. Was he following her? Nancy wondered. Or were the two headed for the same destination?

Determined to find out, Nancy threw the last of her cone in the trash, then jogged after them. A group of teenagers, boom boxes blaring, was headed toward the band.

"Excuse me, excuse me," Nancy called out, weaving through the throng. She was so intent on keeping Janie and Karl in sight that she ran smack into a baby stroller, nearly tipping it.

"Oh!" Nancy righted the stroller, and the baby

burst out crying. "Watch where you're going, young lady," the woman pushing it scolded.

"I'm so sorry!" Nancy said. When she finally got away, she'd lost Janie and Karl.

Frustrated, she smacked her fist in her palm. She noted that they were headed toward Pier Three. Were they going to the ship? Should she go after them?

The shrill blare of police sirens coming from the direction of the hotel cut into her thoughts. Could there have been another burglary? Nancy wondered.

For an instant, Nancy didn't move, frozen with indecision. Finally the sirens won out, and she took off for the Harborside. Three police cars had pulled up in front.

She jogged into the lobby, straight for the desk clerk. "What's going on?"

"Nothing, miss," the clerk said evasively.

"Nothing?" Nancy repeated. "Three police cars are nothing?"

The clerk glanced around, then leaned across the desk. "Robbery in the penthouse suite."

"Thanks." Nancy dashed into the elevator and punched P. When the door opened at the top floor, she peered down the hallway.

The hallway was elegantly decorated with cut-velvet wallpaper against a gold background. An antique table stood against one wall with a vase of fresh flowers on it. Beyond the end table, Nancy could see light spilling from an open doorway onto the Oriental runner.

She stepped into the hall and headed for the open door. Immediately, a uniformed officer appeared and held up his hand to stop her.

"I need to talk to Detective Weller," Nancy explained, trying to see over the officer's shoulder.

"This is official police business," the officer said. "No bystanders allowed."

"That must mean the suite was robbed," Nancy pressed. "Does it look like the same thief?"

"The officer in charge will make a statement in a few minutes. You can watch it on tonight's news." Taking her by the elbow, the police officer was steering her to the elevator when Nancy saw Weller step from the suite.

"Detective Weller!" Nancy called.

"Ms. Drew." He came right over. "Just the person I need."

Nancy's brows shot up. "I am?"

"Thank you, officer," Weller said, guiding Nancy into the elevator. "Yes, I have something you'll want to see." He punched the button, taking Nancy to the next floor down. When they stepped from the elevator, Nancy realized the floor held offices instead of guest rooms.

"Right this way," Weller said, opening a door

and gesturing for her to go inside. A man sat in a swivel chair in front of a wall of TV screens. Nancy looked closer at the screens, realizing they showed different areas in the hotel.

"This is Rolf de Jagger, chief of hotel security," Weller said. "Play her the tape of the penthouse suite, Rolf."

Rolf stuck a tape into a video machine, then punched the play button. When a black-and-white picture flashed on one of the TV screens, Nancy recognized the hall outside the penthouse suite. The suite door was open, just as it had been when she was there.

Suddenly, two figures burst from the open doorway and ran down the hall, disappearing from view.

"Play it again for her, Rolf," Weller said.

But Nancy didn't need to see the tape again. She knew exactly who had charged from the suite: Anne Bonny and Calico Jack Rackham.

7

Shaky Alibis

The pair running down the hall were costumed just like George and Daniel had been at dress rehearsal earlier that afternoon.

Only it can't be, Nancy thought angrily. There has to be some mistake.

"So what do you think?" Detective Weller asked. Arms folded, he rocked back on his heels, a slightly smug expression on his face.

Nancy gave him a cool look. "I think you're showing me this surveillance video for a reason, but I'm not sure what it is."

Weller dropped his arms. "Quit playing dumb, Ms. Drew. You know who these two pirates are. It'll be a lot easier for everybody if you just tell us now instead of making us spend all night interrogating everyone in the cast and crew all over again."

"I'm still curious why you let me see the video," Nancy said.

"I called Chief McGinnis. He says you're legitimate. I figured since you're a detective, you'd want to help us solve these burglaries."

Nancy thought about what he had said, then looked back at the monitor. "Could you freeze the tape on the fleeing thieves?" she asked de Jagger.

When he did, Nancy studied the pirates in the hall. They were about the same size as Daniel and George. But Calico Jack had pulled his tricornered hat low on his forehead, and Anne Bonny had tied a bandanna around her mouth and jaw. There was no way Nancy could positively identify them.

She shook her head. "I can't tell who they are."

Weller bent over so his face was close to hers. "You don't need to. Just tell us who plays these characters in that film you're making."

Nancy held her ground. "I could do that, but *they* didn't burglarize the suite."

"We don't want to arrest them," Weller said patiently. "We want to talk to them. Besides, how do you know they *didn't* do it? Whoever burglarized the suite was as swift and cunning as a real pirate. This time they got in and out at ten, when the hotel was busy with people. The closest thing to a pirate around here is the actors on your ship."

Nancy took a deep breath. "I know it wasn't them because the pirate with the bandanna is Anne Bonny. My friend George plays Anne in the film, and I know for certain that the thief"—she tapped the TV monitor—"is not George."

Weller straightened, a pensive look on his face as he studied Nancy. "How can you be so certain?"

"One reason is that she has an alibi for last night when the other rooms were burglarized. Me."

"You were asleep, Ms. Drew," Weller reminded her.

"The second reason is that my friend George would *never* break the law."

Without commenting, Weller turned back to the screen. "Who's the other pirate?"

"Calico Jack Rackham. The actor who plays him is Daniel Wagner. He and his twin brother, Andrew, own Seeing Double Productions, the company producing the film."

"I remember him. Kind of pompous."

"George and Daniel were together tonight," Nancy added. "They went to dinner and Fort McHenry. I'm sure they have tickets and check stubs to prove it. Besides, anyone could have swiped those costumes and posed as the pirates."

"Not anyone," Weller said, escorting her back into the hall.

Nancy realized what he meant. It had to be someone familiar with the ship. Someone from the cast and crew. Much to her dismay, all the evidence was pointing in that direction.

"What was your friend wearing?" Weller asked.

"Jeans, sandals, a vest," Nancy said. "You know, like half the people walking around out there."

Flicking on his walkie-talkie, Weller radioed his officers, giving them a description of Daniel and George.

"What next?" Nancy asked as the two headed for the elevator.

Weller pressed the down button. "I'm going to the ship to find those costumes."

"Good, I'll go with you. I can help you find them faster." The doors opened, and Nancy stepped into the elevator. Weller had a grim look on his face, but he didn't say she couldn't go with him.

An unmarked police car was sitting in the valet parking area in front of the hotel. Nancy slid into the passenger seat. Weller drove, his gaze intent on the busy roads. The car radio transmitted several messages but he ignored them.

"We could have gotten there faster by walking," Nancy said.

Fifteen minutes later they were boarding the *Swift Adventure*. The ship was dark, lit only by several lanterns. Nancy noticed that all was quiet. Weller had stationed a uniformed officer at the end of the gangplank, giving her orders not to let anyone on or off.

Nancy led Weller into steerage. The door into the Great Cabin was open, and she could hear voices. Striding past Nancy, Weller went straight to the cabin.

Andrew and Harold were sitting at a small table, looking at a drawing of the deck of the ship. Nancy knew they used the drawing to help plan their camera setups.

Weller announced himself with a brusque "Good evening, Mr. Wagner, Mr. Oates. Can you gentlemen tell me where you were all evening?"

Looking up, Andrew stared at the detective, and Harold blinked in surprise.

"What do you want to know that for?" Andrew asked. Nancy thought he sounded defensive.

"Just answer the question, please." Weller flipped open his pad.

"I had dinner with Karl Kidd at about seven," Harold said. "Then I went back to my room and watched a movie on TV until Andrew called me around ten-thirty."

"Where are you staying, and what's your room number?" Weller asked. After Harold gave him the information, Weller turned his attention to Andrew.

Nancy thought the twin looked slightly flustered. "I was here all night working on changes in the script," he said.

"Anyone with you?" Weller asked.

"Not until Harold got here, around eleven."

That meant neither of them had alibis for the time of the robbery, Nancy realized.

Weller thanked them. "I'll be talking with you later. May I take a look in your dressing room?"

Andrew stood up. "What for? Are you still hunting for gold?"

"Costumes this time. We had another robbery in the hotel." Turning, he went down the passageway to the dressing room.

Nancy went inside first, heading to the pegs on the wall. "George and Daniel keep their costumes right—" Her voice trailed off as she sorted through the various articles of clothing hanging from the pegs. George's shirt and trousers and Daniel's naval jacket were not among them.

By then Andrew was standing in the passageway, his face red. "Will someone tell me what is going on? What does a robbery at the hotel have to do with our costumes?"

Just then Weller's pager went off. "Excuse me," he said, then quickly left.

When he was gone, Nancy told Andrew everything. "Weller suspects someone working on the film," she finished.

Andrew's face went white. "They got the burglars on tape?" he exclaimed.

That's an odd response, Nancy thought. She would have expected him to protest that there was no way someone from the ship was involved.

"Yes," Nancy said. "That means Detective Weller is going to turn this ship upside down until he finds some evidence pointing to who they are."

Andrew exhaled loudly, but his face was expressionless. Nancy couldn't tell what he was thinking. If he was involved, he had to be seriously worried.

"I'm going to check the other cabins for the costumes," Nancy finally said. "If they're gone, it may mean our mysterious snooper took them. That *might* clear everybody from the ship."

"What mysterious snooper?" Andrew looked puzzled.

Nancy reminded him about finding the shoe box of spilled doubloons.

"Right." Frowning, he glanced over his shoulder. Harold had come into the passageway. The two went back into the Great Cabin, talking. Nancy listened, but Andrew was only repeating her story about the theft.

By the time Weller came back onboard, Nancy had searched every room that cast and crew had access to, including the cargo area. There was no sign of either costume.

"I can't find the clothing anywhere," she told Weller. "That doesn't mean they aren't stashed somewhere else—like the bow, where the tourist groups are still able to visit."

"Don't worry about it. The officers found your friend," Weller said. "She's waiting for us in your room."

"Good, I'm sure she can clear this up once and for all," Nancy said confidently.

The two hurried back to the hotel. When Nancy went up to their room, George was sitting on the end of her bed, looking confused. A police officer stood outside the door. When George saw Nancy, she jumped up. "Am I glad to see you!"

"Where's Daniel?" Nancy asked.

"He went back to the ship," George said.

"What's he wearing?" Detective Weller asked as he took out his walkie-talkie.

"Why do you want to—?" George began.

"Ms. Fayne," Weller cut in. "What was he wearing?"

"Go ahead and tell him, George," Nancy said, trying to sound reassuring.

"Khaki shorts, sandals, and a 'Baltimore Is for Crabs' T-shirt."

"Kinslow, keep your eye out for the second suspect, Daniel Wagner." Weller gave a description into his walkie-talkie.

"Nancy, what is going on?" George asked. "The police officer was in the hotel lobby when I came back. He acted as if I'd committed a crime or something."

Nancy was opening her mouth to explain when Weller pulled out his pad. "Tell me everything you did, Ms. Fayne, from the time you left the hotel room this evening to the time you arrived and met the officer in the lobby." He tapped the pad with his pen.

George shot Nancy a puzzled look. "It's okay," Nancy told her.

"Well, I met Daniel in the lobby," George said, sinking down on the bed. "We walked to Fort McHenry—"

"Do you have the ticket stubs?" Nancy asked.

George shook her head. "We were having such a good time talking and going over our lines, we decided not to go in."

"What about dinner?" Nancy pressed. "You must have eaten at a restaurant. Did you get a—?"

"Excuse me, Ms. Drew," Weller cut in. *"I'm* interviewing your friend. If you break in again, you'll have to wait out in the hall."

"I'm sorry." Folding her arms against her

chest, Nancy crossed to the other side of the room.

"We didn't eat in a restaurant. Daniel brought a picnic dinner. He just got some stuff at Harborplace." George gave Nancy an uneasy look. Nancy smiled reassuringly at her friend, though inside she was worried. So far, George had nothing to prove where the two had been during the time of the robbery.

"Where did you walk? Where did you eat?" Weller asked.

"Uhh . . . I don't know," George replied in a small voice. "We were just kind of exploring the harbor. We sat by some boats docked on a wharf."

"Did anyone see you?"

George shrugged. "Lots of people, but they were all sight-seers, too."

Weller glanced up from his pad. "So you have no one to confirm where you were all night?"

"Of course I do. Daniel was with me," George said.

"Uh-huh, the infamous Calico Jack." Weller nodded as he wrote.

Frowning, George stood up. "Nancy, what is going on? Why am I being interrogated?"

Nancy's gaze darted to Weller. "You need to tell her."

"We have reason to believe that you and your

friend Mr. Wagner were involved in a hotel burglary tonight."

"What!" George blurted. "That's insane."

"That's what I told him," Nancy said. "We'll get this cleared up. Don't worry."

"Ms. Drew," Weller said as he put his pad away. "May I have your permission to look around?"

Nancy knew what he was hunting for. "Yes, we have nothing to hide. And if George says that's where she and Daniel were tonight, then that's exactly where they were."

Nancy could tell Weller wasn't listening. He was wandering around, opening drawers and suitcases. When he went into the bathroom, Nancy quickly told George about the videotape.

Her friend's eyes grew huge. "They think Daniel and I robbed the penthouse suite?" she exclaimed in a low voice. "If the police weren't acting so serious, I'd burst out laughing."

When Weller came out, Nancy asked, "Find anything?"

Without replying, he crouched beside the bed nearer the bathroom and pulled up the bedspread. Ducking, he peered underneath.

"Hmm." He sat back on his heels and drew a latex glove from his jacket pocket. Nancy caught her breath. Had he found something?

After slipping on the glove, he reached under

the bed and pulled out several articles of clothing.

Nancy's heart sank when she saw them. They were the Anne Bonny and Calico Jack costumes. She strode over to the bed. "I don't understand how those got there."

"So you recognize them," Weller said. Standing up, he directed a stern gaze at George, who stood frozen at the end of the bed.

Nancy grabbed his arm. "Wait, you can't possibly think George had anything to do with the burglary!"

"Oh, but I do. The evidence points right to your friend, I'm afraid." Reaching behind him, Weller pulled his handcuffs from his belt pouch. "George Fayne, you're under arrest for the hotel burglaries."

8

A Close Shave

"You can't arrest George. She and Daniel have been set up!" Nancy protested to Detective Weller. "If the burglar has a master key card, he or she could have sneaked into our room and put the costumes under the bed. Neither of us has been here all night."

"Put your hands in front of you, Ms. Fayne," Weller said, holding up the handcuffs.

"Nancy, tell him there's no way I could have burglarized those rooms." George's face had turned pale.

"I already have," Nancy said. "He knows he's making a big mistake."

"I have no choice," Weller told them. "The evidence is stacked against your friend." Taking

82

hold of George's arm, he snapped the cuffs around her right wrist, then her left wrist.

"Officer Reaves," he barked. "Escort these ladies to my office and start processing Ms. Fayne. I want fingerprints, photos, the works. I'm going to pick up Mr. Wagner."

"Nancy," George whispered in a frightened voice as Officer Reaves came into the hotel room. "This can't be happening."

Nancy squeezed her friend's shoulder. "Don't worry. I'll get you out of this," she said, trying to sound more confident than she felt.

The videotape and the stashed costumes were very incriminating, Nancy realized. She knew she'd have to do some fast investigating to prove that George was innocent.

Nancy shifted in the chair at the police station, trying to get comfortable. It was six o'clock on Wednesday morning, and she'd been dozing on and off since George had been brought in. About half an hour after they'd arrived, Daniel had been escorted into the station by two police officers. Before he even saw Nancy, he'd been whisked into a separate office for interviewing.

Sitting up, Nancy rubbed the crick in her neck. She hadn't spoken to anyone since George had been arrested. Obviously, Weller was avoiding her. Whenever he saw her, he headed in the opposite direction.

Earlier, Nancy had called her father, Carson Drew, who said he'd take the first plane to Baltimore if George needed him. Nancy thanked him, but told him that first she wanted to find out for sure if George had been charged with a crime.

"Ms. Drew?" Detective Weller came down the hall, a coffee mug in his hand. He'd taken off his jacket, loosened his tie, and rolled up the sleeves of his now-wrinkled shirt. When he drew closer, Nancy noticed how bloodshot his eyes were.

She straightened in her seat. "Are you finally going to tell me what's going on?"

"Your friends are being released. We didn't charge them with anything."

"Thank goodness." Relieved, Nancy sank back in the chair for a second before asking, "What made you change your mind?"

"We lifted a fingerprint from the penthouse suite that matched a print belonging to Chance Curran, a cat burglar who has committed a string of robberies up and down the East Coast in the past two years."

"A cat burglar? And you don't suspect George and Daniel at all?" Nancy asked.

"Curran has been known to work with a female accomplice, but since none of the prints we found in the suite match either one of your friends', we're letting them go."

"So George and Daniel were set up, just as I said," Nancy told him.

Weller shrugged. "We don't know for sure. The thieves could have been wearing gloves, and Curran left a print by accident."

"If you have prints on this Curran guy, why hasn't he been picked up?" Nancy asked.

Weller rubbed the bridge of his nose with two fingers as if he had a headache. "The prints are from Curran's first arrest. Since he had no prior record—not even a parking ticket—he didn't serve any jail time. He was put on probation for a year, during which time he stayed clean—at least we think he stayed clean. That's the last time he was ever caught."

"How do you know he's behind the other thefts?" Nancy asked.

"Fingerprints. It seems he always leaves one behind. Like a calling card to taunt us."

"Then why haven't you caught him?"

"This is the first time he's hit Baltimore," Weller said quickly. "He's a master of disguise— he changes his looks and identity every place he goes. He's also smart. He cases out a place carefully—somehow blending in so no one suspects him. His first heist was at a ski resort in Vermont. Two months later, he hit a New York City hotel. Before he came to Baltimore, he burglarized a casino in Atlantic City, New Jersey.

He's quick to get in and out, another reason the police haven't caught up with him."

"Sounds like he's working his way down the East Coast," Nancy said, then she tapped her lip with one finger. "One thing is different about the Baltimore burglaries. This time he hit the Harborside Hotel *twice.*"

"Very observant, Ms. Drew. He's either getting bold or careless."

A rush of anger filled Nancy as she realized why Chance Curran had changed his MO—his method of operation. "I'd say he's feeling bold because somehow he was able to pin the blame on George and Daniel, am I right?"

"That's what we think." Weller took a sip of his coffee, then sat down wearily in the chair next to Nancy's. "Which brings me to you, Ms. Drew. We need your help."

Nancy already had an idea what the detective wanted her to do. "You think that Chance Curran is connected to the ship and the film."

"Correct. The doubloons and costumes could only have been taken by someone with access to all the areas of the ship."

"Plus, the person had to know what George and Daniel were wearing," Nancy added. "What do you want me to do?"

"We want you to get some fingerprints for us," Weller explained. "If the lab techs even go near the ship, Curran's going to run. We've asked

George and Daniel to pretend they're still under investigation. We're hoping Curran's going to be so cocky, he'll stick around, maybe even make a mistake."

"He's already made a *big* mistake." Nancy stood abruptly, all her fatigue gone. "He framed two of my friends. If Curran's on that ship, I'll find him."

"Take one, scene four," Nancy announced as she snapped the slate in front of the camera. It was nine o'clock the same morning. George had gone back to the room to shower and sleep. Even though Nancy was exhausted, she'd forced herself to come onboard for the morning's shoot.

She was glad she had. Already she'd collected a coffee cup with Harold's prints and a pen with Andrew's. She carefully placed the objects in paper evidence bags and stashed them in a small backpack she'd borrowed from George. Then she'd stowed the backpack in the dressing room. Now, if she could only get Eli's and Karl's . . .

"Action!" Andrew called from his stool. He sat beside Lian, who was operating the camera.

Blackbeard strode across the deck to the ship's wheel. He was dressed in black hat, black cape, and high black boots. A gray cloud billowed from under his broad-brimmed hat.

Nancy had read all about Blackbeard and his fierce appearance. Before attacking an enemy ship, he would light cannon wicks and stick them under his hatband. Holding pistols in both hands, he would leap onto the enemy ship, roaring loudly. The effect usually sent the enemy running.

For safety's sake, Eli had placed dry ice in Karl Kidd's hatband instead of real wicks. With his bristly beard, bushy brows, and nasty scowl, Kidd could have passed for the real Blackbeard.

Nancy tried to picture Karl in Calico Jack's costume. Karl was larger than Daniel, but the baggy clothes would still have fit. And since his face had been shadowed by the hat, Nancy hadn't been able to tell if the person in the video had a beard.

Her eyes strayed to Janie, who was adjusting an extra's sailor costume. Nancy hadn't gotten a chance to ask Janie where she and Karl had been going the night of the burglary. Were the two rushing from the hotel after committing the burglary? Nancy thought it was a distinct possibility.

"Raise the Jolly Roger!" Blackbeard thundered, drawing Nancy's attention back to the set. "Prepare to board! Take no prisoners!" he bellowed to an imaginary group of sailors as he leaped on top of a cannon, brandishing his two pistols.

To the left of Blackbeard, Harold Oates raised a reflective shield, focusing the light on Karl's face. Nancy knew that even when they filmed during the day, they needed extra light to make sure the actors' faces weren't in shadow.

Nancy took the opportunity to study Harold—who also didn't have an alibi for the night of the burglary, Nancy thought. Harold was thinner than Daniel, but the bulky costume would have disguised his shape.

Then there was Eli, who was passing out swords and muskets for the boarding scene. Five-foot-eight with skinny arms, Eli was hardly the daring cat burglar type. Still, Detective Weller had said Curran made it a point to blend in so no one noticed him. That described both crew members well.

Nancy's thoughts drifted to Andrew, who was showing Lian where to move the camera for a second take. He hadn't been overly concerned when she'd told him about Daniel being arrested. In fact, all he'd said was "I hope he's here when *Good Morning Baltimore* shows up."

So much for brotherly love, Nancy thought. Or was *Andrew* really Chance Curran, and his plan all along was for suspicion to be thrown onto his brother? Nancy already knew he needed money and publicity for the film. The thefts had accomplished both. The question was, would Andrew sacrifice his brother for a movie?

Nancy hugged the slate, her thoughts in turmoil. No one seemed to fit the role of cat burglar.

But then if Curran was clever enough to frame George and Daniel, he was clever enough to keep his identity a secret.

"Nancy!" someone called.

Startled, she jerked her head around. Everybody was looking at her. "What?"

"Are we interrupting an exciting daydream?" Andrew teased.

She flushed. "No. I just didn't get any sleep last night, and I guess I'm spacing out."

Janie bustled over, a concerned look on her face. "Andrew, let her go back to the hotel and take a nap."

"All right," Andrew agreed. "Go get some shut-eye. But you and George be back here this afternoon at two for the *Good Morning Baltimore* team," he added, pointing a pen in her direction.

"Fine." Nancy handed Janie the slate, then hurried from the quarterdeck. This would be the perfect opportunity to get something with Karl's prints on it, she thought. If only she could find an object he wouldn't miss.

She glanced at her watch before jumping down the steps into steerage. Almost ten. If she hurried, she could get a few hours of sleep.

When she reached the dressing room, Nancy went straight to the pegs on the wall where Karl had hung his street clothes that morning. She lifted his shirt off the peg. His buttons might have a partial print, but he was bound to notice if his shirt was missing.

Next she checked his jeans, rifling the pockets, hoping to find spare change, a comb, anything that might hold a print. They were empty.

Nancy blew out a frustrated breath. Her gaze landed on his belt. Of course! The metal buckle would be a perfect place to find a print.

Careful not to touch the buckle, Nancy began to pull the belt from the loops. The squeak of a floorboard made her glance over her shoulder.

Karl Kidd filled the dressing room doorway, a murderous expression on his face. Without a word, he raised his hand and hurled a dagger straight at Nancy's head!

9

A Fishy Assailant

Nancy ducked. The dagger whistled over her head, whacking into the ship wall.

"What was that for!" Nancy yelled at Karl, her arms rigid by her sides. "You could've killed me!"

Throwing back his head, he burst out laughing. "You're right, I could have, but I didn't."

More angry than frightened, Nancy whirled and reached for the dagger. In one long stride, Karl crossed the dressing room and grabbed her wrist before she could get it.

"In fact, I didn't touch a hair on your head, did I?" he growled. "Now, why don't you explain why you were going through my pants pockets?"

Nancy gritted her teeth, angry that she'd been

caught. If Karl was really Curran, she knew she'd better think of a good answer.

"I didn't know they were your pants," she said tightly. "Eli sent me down to get a belt for one of the extras. He told me the belt was in a pair of jeans. Now let me go."

She could feel Karl's hot breath on the top of her head. Would he believe her?

Using his other hand, he reached up and pulled the dagger from the wall. Then he let go of her wrist.

Turning, she met his hard stare. His hat was pulled low on his forehead, his black hair hung lank on his shoulders, and his lips were curled in a sneer of disbelief.

"Maybe you need to take a break from playing Blackbeard," she said. "You're starting to act like him."

Karl cocked a dark brow, a wicked gleam in his eye. "Thank you," he said. Without taking his eyes off her, he stuck his dagger in his waist sash.

"What are *you* doing down here?" Nancy asked, crossing her arms in front of her.

"I had a minute's break before they shot the third take. Janie told me I needed to blacken my teeth." He flashed her a huge grin. "They were just too white and pretty whenever I called, 'Hang the varmints from the yardarm!' "

Stepping back, he gestured toward the open doorway with a mock bow. "After you, ma'am."

Nancy picked up the backpack, squared her shoulders, and marched past him. When she reached the passageway, she ran up the steps to the waist. Once she was safely outside in the sunlight, she exhaled in relief.

That was a close call. Karl Kidd could easily be Curran, she thought. Not only was he arrogant and smart, he had all the right moves. Hadn't he boasted that the burglaries were the work of a crafty bunch of pirates? she thought.

As she walked down the gangplank, a slow smile spread over her face. Of course, he wasn't quite smart enough to beat her.

Raising her arm, Nancy looked at her wrist. Maybe she hadn't gotten Karl Kidd's buckle, but when he'd grabbed her arm, he'd left clear prints on the band of her watch. As soon as Weller could process the prints, she'd know for sure if Karl Kidd was Chance Curran.

Riiiiing. The incessant whine forced its way into Nancy's brain. Reaching out blindly, she flung her hand in the direction of the bedside table, finally swatting the top button on the clock radio.

A groan came from the other bed. "Don't tell me it's afternoon already."

Opening one eye, Nancy looked over at George, who'd pulled the covers over her head to keep the afternoon sun out of her eyes. "Hey, you had more sleep than I did, so quit complaining," she said, her sentence broken by a yawn.

"That may be true, but you didn't have the humiliating experience of being treated like a common criminal." George tossed the sheet off her face. "What time did you finally get here? I didn't hear you come in."

"That's because you were snoring too loud." Nancy stifled a grin.

As soon as she'd gotten to the hotel room, she'd called Weller, showered, and then delivered the evidence bags to an officer who had met her in the lobby. Finally, she'd crawled into bed and fallen promptly asleep. Through all the commotion, George hadn't budged.

"How was the shoot this morning?" George asked, sounding more awake. "Did anyone even wonder why Daniel and I weren't there?"

"You weren't supposed to be there, remember?" Nancy reminder her. "They aren't shooting your scene until this afternoon. Still, I told Janie and Andrew about the arrest. Janie acted totally shocked. Andrew, on the other hand, wanted to know if you'd make it this afternoon."

George snorted. "So much for sympathy."

"It didn't take long for the story to get around to all the cast and crew members. I made it sound as if you and Daniel are still prime suspects."

Sitting up in bed, George hugged her legs. "Then I guess we'll see how good an actor Daniel really is. He's going to have to play the part of the wrongfully accused victim."

"I think he'll give an award-winning performance. Talking about performances—" Nancy told George all about her encounter with Karl Kidd.

"Wow, if he'd come after me, I would have been shaking in my Anne Bonny boots," George said.

"I was pretty scared," Nancy admitted, then grinned triumphantly. "But I got his prints! As well as Andrew's and Harold's."

"How long will it take Weller to run them?"

"He says there's a backlog, but because Chance Curran is wanted by several other police departments in different states, they're making this case a priority."

Throwing back the covers, Nancy got out of bed, her energy returning. She grabbed her clothes off the back of a chair, then went into the bathroom to change and wash up.

"Janie said Andrew's having a big spread for lunch on the ship," Nancy called out to George, "to impress the *Good Morning Baltimore* crew. If we hurry, there might be something left."

"Then let's hurry!" George called back. "I'm starving."

Half an hour later, they were walking down Pier Three toward the *Swift Adventure*. Nancy turned to go up the gangplank when she noticed

Selena strolling across the bridge they'd just crossed. She was walking arm-in-arm with a man.

"George." Nancy nudged her friend. "Don't stare, but can you tell whom Selena is with?"

George nonchalantly glanced toward the bridge. "He doesn't look like anyone from the film, but whoever he is, they seem cozy."

When Nancy reached the main deck, she sneaked a peek over the railing. Instantly, she realized who the man was—Joseph Mascelli.

"She's with that reporter I caught in the cargo hold," Nancy told George.

George chuckled. "She must be giving him a very intimate interview."

"Really." Nancy furrowed her brow. "This whole publicity thing has gotten out of hand. I wish I could figure out how it ties in with the burglaries."

"On two hours of sleep, I'm surprised you can tie your own shoes," George said with a chuckle.

When they climbed up the ladder to the quarterdeck, Nancy spotted Scott Harlow, the waiter from the hotel dining room. He was talking to Janie, an earnest expression on his face.

"I'd forgotten Janie invited Scott," Nancy said, waving. When he saw them, his eyes brightened. Nancy pointed to the buffet table, then made a motion as if she were eating. He nodded as if he understood.

Picking up a plate, she got in line with George.

"Remember to keep your ears and eyes open," she whispered as she piled her plate high with homemade rolls and salads. "The real thief is probably checking you out right this minute."

George grinned before popping a grape into her mouth. "Good," she said. "Anne Bonny can handle anything."

Just then Eli bustled over. "I've got a new costume for you to try on," he said to George. "Since the *police* took the other one."

"Nancy!" Lian rushed over. "This next scene requires a ton of camera angles. You're going to need—"

As the two rattled on, Nancy and George shot each other wry looks. The afternoon was going to be a busy one.

"That's a wrap!" Andrew called four hours later. "Thank you, everyone. Take the night off and enjoy yourselves."

"Whew." George gasped as she pulled her scarf off her head. "Did he say take the night off?"

Nancy was bent over picking up muskets, pistols, swords, and daggers that had fallen during a fight scene. Before the shoot, she and Eli had laid canvas on top of the deck so it wouldn't get splattered with the fake blood.

"Yes, and the words were music to my ears. I'm going to sleep—" Nancy began.

"Nancy, George," Janie called. "Lian and I are going to the aquarium after we pack up. How about coming with us? It might be our last chance to sightsee."

Nancy straightened, her arms full of props. "Sounds like a good idea," she said. "George, what do you think? We can still get to bed early."

"Count me in," George said. "I just need to change." Taking a few swords from Nancy, she headed for the steerage deck. Lian and Janie went to pack up cameras and lights.

Nancy looked around the quarterdeck. The cast had gone to change, the *Good Morning Baltimore* crew had finished their taping, and Scott had left to go to work. Without the extras, the ship almost seemed quiet.

Nancy's gaze rested on Janie and Lian. Weller had said that Curran worked with a female accomplice. Nancy realized there was always a chance she was on the ship right now—working side by side with her.

But could the pair be Janie and Lian? Nancy shook her head, not wanting to believe either could be involved. She liked them both. Still, maybe the aquarium would be a good place to pump them casually for information.

A girlish laugh drew Nancy's attention to the waist below. Selena and Joseph were leaving the ship. The reporter had his arm around Selena's shoulder. Throughout the afternoon's shoot, he'd stayed onboard, sometimes taking notes, but usually with his attention on Selena.

And why not? Nancy thought as she watched Selena sashay down the gangplank in her spike heels and low-cut dress. Selena was beautiful, and when Joseph was around, she played the charming actress. Nancy had to wonder what other roles she could play. Was thief in her repertoire?

"Wow, look at that shark!" Lian exlaimed as the four girls walked up the spiral ramp of the aquarium's Open Ocean exhibit. "The only thing that separates us from his gaping jaws is that little bitty thickness of glass."

"It really does feel like you're underwater with them," George said. "That's because we're surrounded by water. There are two tanks circling us. The one at this level holds sharks. Above us is the Atlantic Coral Reef."

Janie and Lian had stopped to watch another shark lazily swimming past. "How do you know so much about the aquarium?" Janie asked, glancing at George over her shoulder.

"Nancy and I were here once before on a—"

Nancy poked George in the side with her elbow. "—on a tour," she cut in hastily, not wanting George to mention anything about being detectives.

"Oh, look at that!" Lian exclaimed. The three girls turned their attention back to the glass-enclosed tank. Nancy glanced at her wrist, then remembered that the police had her watch. "What time is it, George?"

"Twenty minutes before the whale and dolphin show starts."

"I'm going to find a place to sit down for a minute," Nancy told the others. "The lack of sleep is catching up to me. Meet you by the Children's Cove."

They waved, and Nancy continued up the ramp, hunting for a bench. When she reached the Children's Cove, several groups of kids were clustered around the touch pool. Nancy walked around slowly, letting her mind wander. So far, neither Janie nor Lian had said or done anything suspicious. Perhaps the female accomplice had nothing to do with the film and ship.

Nancy walked over to the Tide Pool just as a crowd of children left. She leaned over to check out the urchins and anemones. Do Not Touch, the sign said. These sea creatures can sting.

"And so can I," a voice hissed menacingly in Nancy's ear as she felt a sharp prick in her side.

10

A Message in Blood

"Don't turn around," the person whispered hoarsely, "or you'll regret it." Nancy winced as the sharp point pressed against her flesh. "Now walk to the door to your left that says Employees."

Without moving her head, Nancy looked at the door. Knowing the layout of the aquarium, she figured it led to a stairwell. She knew that it would be crazy to enter a dark, empty stairwell with a knife-wielding thug.

Nancy spotted the escalator that went up to the rain forest exhibit. If she could just get to it, she knew she might be able to get away.

"Mom, look!" Several children pushed their way toward the Tide Pool. Twisting her body sideways, Nancy knocked her elbow into the person behind her, sending the knife clattering across the floor.

Without hesitating, Nancy took off. It was too dangerous to go after the person or the knife. In the milling crowd of children, someone could get hurt.

Pushing past two teenagers, she leaped onto the escalator and started climbing. She glanced behind her, but the escalator moved her out of view before she could glimpse her attacker.

When she reached the rain forest exhibit, Nancy raced along the wooden walkways. The steamy air made her break into a sweat. Or was it the close call that had her perspiring? Should she contact security? They could watch the exits to try to nab the attacker.

Whom would she tell them to look for, though? Nancy wondered. She'd been so intent on escaping without anyone getting hurt that she hadn't seen the person. The only thing she might recognize was the voice, which was low and hoarse like a man's—or a woman trying to sound like a man, Nancy thought ruefully.

Darting around a cluster of tourists, Nancy made her way from the rain forest, down the escalator on the other side, and back to the ring tanks. George, Lian, and Janie should be waiting at the top to meet me, she thought.

She spotted George staring at the puffins.

"Come look, they're so cute!" her friend called, waving. When she saw Nancy's face, her smile turned to a frown. "Are you all right?"

"I'm okay—now. I'll fill you in later. Where are Lian and Janie?" Nancy said quickly.

"We split up. Janie wanted to get something to drink before the dolphin show, and Lian headed to the gift shop. They're going to meet us at the amphitheater. Why?"

Drawing George aside, Nancy told her about the person at the Tide Pool.

"What do you think he wanted?" George asked.

"I don't know. Don't you think it's strange that both Lian and Janie left soon after I did?"

George's eyes opened wide. "Oh my gosh. Do you think one of them is Curran's accomplice?"

"It's possible." Nancy paced in front of the puffin exhibit. "What's really scary is that the thieves obviously know I'm after them. But how could they know? We've been so careful!"

George bit her lip. "Weller said that Curran was smart."

"But only you, me, the police, and Daniel know—" Nancy eyes narrowed. *"Daniel."*

"No. No way." George shook her head vehemently.

"Wait a minute, George. I'm not saying he's guilty." Nancy put her hand on her friend's arm. "But what if somehow he let it slip that I'm helping the police? Think how hard it would be to keep a secret from your own brother."

"You still suspect Andrew?" George asked.

"I suspect everybody," Nancy said. "Come on, we need to meet Lian and Janie. I want to see which one looks guiltier."

Nancy led the way down the ramp to the escalator that took them to the Marine Mammal Pavilion. She was glad she had been at the aquarium before and knew her way around.

When they reached the Mammal Pavilion, Nancy spotted Lian and Janie in front of the theater doors. Janie was sipping a soda. Lian was showing her a stuffed seal she'd pulled from an aquarium shopping bag.

Nancy frowned. The two looked totally innocent. Was she wrong to suspect them? she wondered.

"Hey, Nan." Janie waved. "How was the Tide Pool?"

"How did you know I was there?" Nancy asked, her tone sharp.

Janie arched one brow. "That's where George said she was going to meet you."

Lian put her stuffed seal back into the bag. "We'd better go in. The show's about to start."

"Lian just got here, too," Janie said to Nancy as she opened the theater door for everyone.

"There were so many cute animals to choose from," Lian explained.

As they went inside, Nancy glanced at Lian. She had obviously been to the gift shop, then hurried to meet them. But she could also have managed to follow Nancy. Nancy decided not to rule out anyone for the moment.

The four girls made their way to an empty row of seats. Already the jumbo screen was showing scenes of sea mammals. Nancy settled back, her eyes on the screen. But she couldn't stop her mind from racing.

Who had accosted her in the aquarium? Lian? Janie? Or was it someone who had followed them from the ship? And what had been his or her intent?

An involuntary shiver raced up Nancy's arms. She knew what the person had wanted—to scare her, or worse. I must be getting close to blowing Chance's identity, she thought.

Then a new possibility worked its way into Nancy's thoughts. Weller had said that Curran's pattern was to rob and run. That meant something was keeping him here. Something important enough to keep him from fleeing, even though he knew Nancy was getting close.

Was he planning a bigger heist? Or if he was connected to the film, was he going to leave when they finished shooting?

Nancy wasn't sure. But one thing she did

know: from now on, she couldn't let down her guard for a second.

"I'll have the pasta," Nancy said to Scott. Frowning, he wrote her order below George's order of hamburger and fries.

"No seafood tonight?" Scott asked them.

George and Nancy laughed. "No way," George said. "I'd keep thinking it was a cousin of some fish I'd met at the aquarium."

"Oh, right." Scott nodded knowingly, then jerked his thumb to the right. "Think she'll give me an autograph?"

Nancy looked in the direction he was referring to. Selena sat at a private, candlelit table by herself. "I thought you wanted an autograph for *John*," she teased.

He flushed pink. "Right. Uh, he got one already. He's their waiter."

"*Their* waiter?" George asked.

Then Nancy saw a man walking toward the table. Since his back was to her, she wasn't sure who it was, but she figured it must be Joseph Mascelli. When he sat down, she realized it was Andrew. Leaning across the table, he said something to Selena that made her throw back her head and laugh.

"Whoa," George said. "Selena and Andrew? They look mighty friendly."

"Want me to find out what they're discussing?" Scott asked, giving the two girls a conspiratorial wink. "John will be glad to tell all."

"Go for it," Nancy said.

When Scott left, she sat back in her chair. George had dark circles under her eyes. She'd propped her head up with one hand as if too tired to hold it straight. Nancy knew how her friend felt.

"As soon as dinner's over, we'll hit the sack," Nancy promised.

"I know it's only eight, but it feels like midnight," George mumbled. "I can't believe Janie and Lian are off to meet a bunch of the cast and crew at Fells Point."

"At least that's where they said they were going." For a second Nancy played with her fork, her thoughts drifting to Andrew and Selena. Their dinner was probably totally innocent, a chance to discuss script changes. Then again . . .

"A bigger role," Scott said when he brought their salads.

"No thanks, this roll's big enough," George said, pointing to the one on her side plate.

Nancy and Scott laughed. "He means Selena wants a bigger role in the film," Nancy explained.

"Oh. How'd you know that's what he meant?" George asked Nancy.

"Because Scott had that I'm-on-a-case look in his eyes when he brought our salad. And it made sense—Selena definitely would like to be *the star*."

"I'll keep pumping John to see if he digs up anything juicier," Scott promised before leaving.

Nancy speared a piece of lettuce with her fork. "Of course," she said to George in a low voice, "they could be talking about committing crimes, and Selena meant she wants a bigger role in the burglaries."

"There's no way Selena's involved," George said.

"How can you be so sure?"

"Because if that had been Selena in the surveillance videotape, she would have struck a pose so security taped her best angle."

Nancy laughed, glad the evening was ending on a light note. Before dinner she'd called Detective Weller from the hotel room. He'd been so concerned when she told him about the attacker in the aquarium, he'd suggested she do no further investigating.

Nancy told him she was already in too deep. He also had said the prints should be processed by the next day. Nancy hoped so. If Chance Curran knew they were closing in, he could run any minute.

After dinner Nancy and George swung by

Andrew's and Selena's table before heading for their room. The two were still talking as they sipped coffee.

"You two didn't go to Fells Point with the others?" Nancy asked.

Selena rolled her eyes. "Some noisy, crowded restaurant that smells like fish? No thanks. This is more *private.*" She gave Andrew a meaningful look.

"I'll probably join them later," Andrew said, ignoring Selena's look. Nancy wondered if he deliberately did it to annoy the actress, or if he was one of the few men oblivious to her charms.

"We're hitting the sack," George said. "It's been a long crazy day."

Nancy waited, wondering if Andrew would comment on his brother's arrest. When he mentioned shooting the scene instead, she was once again surprised at his lack of interest.

Finally, the two girls said goodbye. "I wonder what it would be like to be as beautiful as Selena," George mused as they took the elevator to their floor. "Men take one look at her and fall hard."

"I don't want men falling at my feet." Nancy stepped out of the elevator. As she and George walked to their room, she glanced up and down the hallway, wondering if the burglars would strike again tonight.

Nancy unlocked the door, and they went inside. "First dibs on the bathroom," Nancy said, pulling a sleep shirt out of her suitcase.

She went into the bathroom, flicked on the light, then gasped. Someone had drawn a crimson heart on the mirror. Beside it was a drawing of a red hourglass. A red liquid seemed to drip from both pictures.

George came rushing in. "What's wro—" She clapped a hand over her mouth when she saw the drawings, their outlines crisscrossing Nancy and George's images in the mirror like bloody slashes.

"Your time is running out," Nancy murmured to herself.

"What?" George gasped.

"That's what the hourglass means." Nancy pointed to it. "It was used on pirate flags to warn other ships."

"And what about the heart?" George asked, her voice cracking.

Nancy inhaled shakily. "That was used on the flags, too. It means, A slow painful death awaits you!"

11

A Narrow Miss

"I don't like the sound of that message," George said. "And I don't like the fact that someone keeps breaking into our room."

"Whoever it is must still have that master key card," Nancy said. "Maybe we'd better move. I'll call the desk and ask them for a new room."

George shuddered. "Good idea. I don't think I could fall asleep thinking some pirate's going to sneak in here tonight and carry out his threat."

"I'm calling Detective Weller, too," Nancy added. "Maybe the police can get some prints off the mirror."

"What is that red stuff anyway?" George asked.

Leaning closer, Nancy studied the goop on the

mirror. "It looks similar to the fake blood we used for the battle scene on the ship."

"Our mysterious prop room bandit again," George observed. "Did you ever get fingerprints from Eli? He has the easiest access to the props."

"No. I wasn't able to get anything he touched without looking obvious. That was a mistake. When you look at the guy, you think there's no way he could be some clever burglar. But that's just the type of person I should be looking for. Chance Curran's gotten away with his crimes because no one's identified him."

Turning, Nancy left the bathroom, George on her heels. "Getting prints from Eli will be my top priority tomorrow," she told George as she picked up the phone to call the lobby desk. "Wimpy Eli Wakefield just may be crafty Chance Curran."

"Do you have any meal receipts from the last couple of days?" Nancy asked Eli on Thursday, the next morning, before filming.

"Don't tell me el cheapo Andrew is reimbursing us for our meals," Eli scoffed as he dug in his pants pockets.

Nancy smiled winningly. "We hope. Publicity has been so good, lots of different broadcasting companies are showing interest in the film."

That's true, Nancy thought as she watched Eli pull out his wallet. "I think I saved several charge receipts from dinners," he said.

Bingo. Nancy tried not to smile too happily. Not only would the police be able to get prints off the receipts, but the receipts should have the date and time on them. Nancy would be able to see if Eli had an alibi for the night she was attacked at the aquarium.

He pulled several crumpled slips of paper from his wallet. "For lunch I grabbed something from a fast food place so I don't have any. I haven't been living too extravagantly."

"So your signature's on the receipts," Nancy observed. She needed to make sure they were identified for the police.

"Right." He gave them to Nancy.

"Thanks," she said brightly. When she moved away, she tucked the receipts into a paper bag along with several others. Hopefully, she'd get a chance to get some good prints from them. They would also help determine where the suspects were the last couple of nights. If they were eating during the time of the robberies or when she was attacked at the aquarium, she could cross them off her list.

Karl Kidd was Nancy's next target. She hadn't talked to him since he'd thrown the dagger at her. Now the big guy was with Janie, who was adjusting his blue uniform jacket. For today's scene Karl was playing the part of Captain Barnet, the man who'd attacked and captured Calico Jack's ship.

Janie had tied Karl's unruly hair back into a

ponytail, trimmed his brows and beard, then sprayed them gray. He almost looked distinguished, Nancy thought.

Nancy approached him when Janie left. He had his knife out and was whittling a small piece of wood.

"Any meal receipts, Karl?" she asked, holding up the paper bag.

Without looking at her, he shook his head no.

"Really? You're missing out on free cash."

He gave her a cold look. "I said I don't have any," he repeated, pointing the knife at her before striding away.

As Nancy watched him go, she wondered about his curious response. Janie came over, a tricornered hat in her hand. "What did you do, scare the captain away?"

"I only asked him if he had receipts," Nancy said. "And he went off in a huff."

"That's odd. Karl should have jumped at the chance for some money. But then the guy's been acting pretty strange since we came to Baltimore."

Nancy turned to face her. "Really?"

"Yeah. When we were doing the Shakespeare production together, Karl was the life of the party. On this film, he's made himself scarce every night."

Nancy tried not to look too interested. "So he wasn't with you guys last night at Fells Point?"

Janie shook her head. "And no one knew where he was, either."

"Strange." Nancy shrugged nonchalantly, though inside her mind was tucking away the interesting information. "Weren't you two together the other night? After you and I had dinner?"

Janie gave her a guarded look. "You must have been mistaken," she said. "Anyway, he's probably been scarce because he has friends in the area that he's been visiting."

"Maybe." Nancy said, backing off when she realized Janie wasn't going to tell her what had really happened.

Janie looked past Nancy, her eyes narrowing. "Oh, goody. Here comes Selena and her puppy dog."

Nancy glanced over her shoulder. Selena was walking across the quarterdeck, Joseph Mascelli tagging behind her.

"At least she's dressed for rehearsal," Janie said with a sigh. "I had to convince her that Mary Read would not be wearing spike heels for the big fight scene."

Nancy burst out laughing. Harold came over carrying the reflective shield. "I'm going to need you to hold this during filming," he told Nancy. "I'll show you where to position it."

"Okay." Nancy tucked the shield under one arm. Folding the bag of receipts, she slid it carefully in the back pocket of her jeans. She would love to rush Eli's prints to the police department, but already actors and crew were gathering for the first take.

George and Daniel came on deck dressed in their new costumes. "What do you think?" George asked, twirling. The sleeves of her rough cotton shirt were ripped, and her baggy pants were held up with a cord. Her teeth had been blackened, her hair tangled, and a red gash ran the length of her cheek.

"I think you should enter the next Miss America contest," Nancy joked.

"Your talent could be fencing," Daniel added, feinting at her with a pretend sword.

"Places!" Janie called. Nancy hurried over to Harold, who showed her where to stand by the railing and how to hold the sheild.

"Mary Read and Anne Bonny will be fighting off Barnet's men," he told her. "Keep the shield on Mary's face. Eli will get Anne's face. When Barnet climbs aboard and Mary shoots him with her pistol, Eli will focus his shield on him."

Nancy nodded, concentrating hard. She saw Andrew signal to Janie, who yelled, "Quiet!"

Standing on a short stepladder, Harold held the boom mike between Anne and Mary. Behind and to the left of Nancy, out of sight of the camera, Karl had straddled the stern railing. When the camera was on him, it would look as if he was boarding the ship.

Darting over to Selena, Janie pulled a strand of hair from her scarf, letting it fall across her face. Selena had also been made up to look grimy and weary, but somehow she still managed to look gorgeous, Nancy noticed.

"Roll sound!" Janie called when she was finished. "Roll camera!" she called a second later, and the camera's red light went on.

"Mark it," Andrew said, and Janie snapped the slate in front of the camera.

"Action," Andrew hollered, and immediately everyone on deck was quiet.

Nancy held the shield steady, trying to make sure Selena's eyes weren't shadowed. Facing each other, Mary Read and Anne Bonny drew their weapons.

"Fire the cannons!" Mary yelled, brandishing a musket.

"Prepare for battle!" Anne yelled, a sword in her hand.

"Surrender or die!" Captain Barnet yelled as he swung onto the deck.

Mary pointed her musket at him. "Never!" she growled, firing.

A boom filled the air and something hit the reflective shield, the blow hurtling Nancy backward. She slammed against the railing, the shield still in her hands.

Screaming hysterically, Selena dropped the smoking pistol.

"Cut!" Andrew cried over the din. Jumping off the stool, he ran over. "What in the world happened?"

"This gun thing really went off!" Selena screeched. Stunned, Nancy stared at the shield still clutched in both hands. A hole had been shot clean through it. When she raised it up again, she realized how close the shot had come to her head.

"Nancy, are you all right?" George came over.

Dropping his shield, Eli bent and picked up the pistol. "That's impossible," he said. "The guns I bought are from a toy store."

Daniel took the weapon from him. "Not this pistol. It's an expert reproduction."

All eyes turned to Selena. "Where did you get it?" Daniel asked.

"Eli gave it to me," Selena said, huge tears running down her cheeks. Nancy had expected Joseph Mascelli to rush over to comfort her. Instead, the reporter was holding out the mike of a tape recorder, trying to get every word.

"Eli," Andrew said in a stern voice. "What's going on?"

Eli shook his head, a confused expression on his face. "I handed her a *fake* pistol for the scene," he declared. "The same kind I gave to Karl."

Nancy glanced toward Karl Kidd. The actor's face was as gray as his beard. Daniel took Karl's pistol and examined it. "This one *is* a cheap fake.

Someone must have switched Selena's. We should call the police."

Andrew groaned. "Not the police. They'll be here all day interrogating us again."

"Yeah, but think of the publicity," Janie said, her tone sarcastic. "In fact, I wouldn't be surprised if Ms. Ramirez pulled this little stunt to get on the front cover of some magazine."

"How dare you say that?" Selena protested, her tears quickly drying up. "That is so wrong."

"Oh, really?" Planting her hands on her hips, Janie stared at Joseph, who was getting ready to take a picture.

Daniel reached out and snatched the camera from him. "Enough! You've already picked our bones clean."

Mascelli shot him a haughty look. "I've just started." Pulling out his pad, he went over to Karl. He flipped back the pages and began to read. "How's this sound for tomorrow's headlines: 'Is the *Swift Adventure* Haunted—With Bad Luck?'" he read. "'Actor Karl Kidd was seen leaving the *Lucky Lady*, a yacht notorious for holding big-stakes card games. Only, sources tell me, Kidd has not been lucky. In fact, he owes so much money, the Big Man's looking for him.'"

"Shut up, Mascelli," Karl growled, and before anyone could stop him, he punched the reporter in the jaw. The blow sent Mascelli sprawling to the deck.

"Joe!" Selena rushed over and knelt beside him. "Are you all right?"

Sitting up, the reporter rubbed his jaw. "You'll pay for this, Kidd."

"I'm already paying. Now get off this ship."

Still rubbing his jaw, Mascelli stood, Selena helping him up, and stalked off.

"What was he talking about, Karl?" Janie asked.

Karl pulled off his hat and ran his fingers through his hair. "Mascelli's right. I got into a card game I shouldn't have with guys way out of my league. They bankrolled me some money. I lost big, and now they want their money back—with interest." He gave Nancy a defeated look. "I'm sorry, Nancy, it's obvious that pistol shot was meant for me—as a warning."

"I'm just glad no one was hurt," Nancy said, knowing he was wrong about the shot being intended for him. There was no way some card shark's goon could have sneaked onboard the ship and replaced the pistols.

Nancy didn't contradict Karl because she didn't want to draw attention to what she figured had really happened. Chance Curran or his accomplice had replaced the pistol, and the shot had been meant for Nancy.

12

A Chance Encounter

If the pistol shot had been meant for her, there was only one person who could have set it up, Nancy thought—Harold! He'd instructed her where to stand so she'd be in Selena's line of fire when the actress aimed at Karl.

Nancy angrily scanned the boat for him. Everybody was milling about, discussing the near-miss. Everybody but Harold. Where had he gone? Nancy wondered.

Then she spotted him on the other side of the wheel, fiddling with his sound equipment. Fists clenched by her sides, Nancy marched toward him.

She caught herself. She wanted whoever was Chance to be arrested and thrown in jail, which meant she had to be patient. She had to wait for the police to match the fingerprints on Harold's cup to Chance Curran's before she was sure he was the culprit.

Still, Detective Weller had said he hoped Chance would get cocky enough to make a mistake. Nancy decided she just might push him in that direction.

When Harold saw her coming, he glanced up. "Gee, Nancy, I'm really sorry about what happened."

"Well, you did kind of set me up," Nancy said, keeping her tone light. "Thank goodness Selena's a lousy shot or Karl or I could've been on our way to the hospital."

"Really." Harold glanced back down at his equipment. Nancy wondered how he could act so innocent and unconcerned. He should be the one getting the acting award, not Selena.

"It's funny, though, how accidents keep happening onboard," Nancy continued. "In fact, the whole haunted ship thing started with you losing your balance and falling overboard."

Harold frowned. "True. Except that *was* just an accident."

"Really?" Nancy drew out the word dramatically.

Harold stopped tinkering and gave her a puzzled look. "Must have been. I mean, why would someone want to whack me in the head with a rope and knock me off the ship?"

"Good question." Nancy tapped her lip. "I was wondering the same thing a minute ago—why would someone want to shoot me?"

"I thought the shot was meant for Karl."

"Was it?" Nancy asked.

"All right, people, let's get ready for take two!" she heard Andrew call behind her. Turning on her heels, Nancy left Harold.

Nancy wished she could get to a phone and call Weller. She wanted to get the receipts to him. She had to find out about the fingerprints.

"Nancy, you mark the scene this time," Andrew said. "We'll let Janie hold the reflective shield."

"You mean you don't mind if *I* get shot?" Janie protested.

"The pistol is not loaded this time," Daniel assured her. "I checked it twice, and so did Harold."

"I'll check it, too," Nancy said quickly. When Daniel handed her the pistol, she could tell instantly that it was the fake. "What did you do with the replica? I really do think the police should see it."

"I locked it in the Great Cabin," Andrew said. "I'll call that Weller guy when we're finished shooting. He can come get it."

The next three takes went without a hitch. When Andrew called for a break, Nancy went over to George. "I need to get to a phone to call Weller myself," she whispered. "I think I know who Chance Curran is!"

George's eyes widened. "Who?"

Nancy put her finger to her lips. "I'll tell you later."

"I remember there's a phone outside the aquarium," George whispered. "Good luck."

Nancy took off at a jog. When she reached the phone, she dug in her pocket for change. Weller wasn't in his office, but the dispatcher said she'd page him.

For five minutes Nancy paced in front of the phone. She couldn't wait to tell Weller she'd found Curran. Finally, it rang. "Detective Weller? Did you find out about the fingerprints? Because I think—" Nancy was about to tell him who the thief was, when Weller cut in, "Got two of them back this morning. No matches."

"Which two?" Nancy asked.

"According to the prints, Harold Oates and Andrew Wagner are *not* Chance Curran. Now, what were you about to tell me?"

Nancy felt deflated. She'd been so sure about Harold. "Nothing. I mean, there is something." She told him about the pistol shot. "If he's telling the truth, Karl Kidd's in big trouble."

"You tell Karl to get in here and talk to the detective who's been trying to shut those card games down," he told her.

"It might mean Karl is Chance. You haven't ruled him out with the prints, right? What if he robbed the rooms to help pay his debt?"

"Possible," Weller agreed. "The thief stole more jewelry and watches than cash. If Kidd's trying to fence the stuff, it may take him a while before he can pay back those goons. And they're not very patient."

Nancy also told Weller about the receipts.

"Good. I'll have an officer pick them up right now. Where are you?"

She gave him her location, then hung up. Sitting dejectedly on the curb, she opened the bag of receipts. When she sorted through them, she noted that there were receipts from everybody except Karl and Selena.

"That's why you have dinner with *men*," the actress had told her. "So you never have to pay for a meal."

Nancy looked over Eli's receipts, checking dates and times. There was no receipt for the night before, which meant he could have been the assailant in the aquarium. She noticed a receipt from the night of the first burglary, but it was for seven o'clock. That meant Eli could still be their thief.

And what about Karl? Was he Curran? Somehow, Nancy couldn't picture the real Chance Curran hanging around long enough to get threatened and shot at by a card shark.

Which brought her back to the same question—why *was* Curran sticking around? Jumping up, she dialed Weller again. "He's planning another heist," she said. "Maybe a bigger one. That's why he and his accomplice are still in Baltimore."

"Could be," Weller agreed. "I'll check around, see if the hotel has anything unusual going on that could be bringing in more money. Why don't I meet you later and go over everything with you?"

"We'll be shooting all morning and afternoon. What about meeting at the hotel lobby around seven?" Nancy suggested.

"Good idea, I'll see you at seven."

A minute later a uniformed officer drove up in a marked police car. Nancy handed over the receipts, then hurried back to the boat. She knew the break would be over. She hoped no one had noticed she'd been gone.

"Celebration dinner seven o'clock at the Seaside Restaurant," Andrew announced to the tired cast and crew. It was late afternoon and filming had finally ended for the day.

"What are we celebrating?" George asked.

Andrew gave everybody a grin. "New backers

for the film. Not only will it be on educational TV, but News Time Productions wants to release it on video!"

Nancy cheered along with the others. Then, taking George aside, she whispered, "I can't go to the dinner. You'll have to tell everybody I already have a date."

"With who?"

"Uh, Scott—" Nancy said the first name who came to mind.

"You do? Where are you going?"

"I don't really have a date with Scott," Nancy whispered. "I'm meeting Detective Weller. He's going over all the receipts and should have more print matches by then. We need to compare notes."

"Got it," George said. "Too bad, though—you'll be missing a fun dinner."

Six o'clock that evening, after George had left, Nancy sat down in the hotel dining room, making sure she was seated in Scott's area. She wanted to grab a sandwich as well as clue him in that he was her excuse for not going to the dinner. She figured he wouldn't mind going along with the ruse.

"I've had enough of the Wagners and their film," Nancy told Scott. "I hope you didn't mind if I told them I was going to be with you."

"Not at all. In fact, why don't we make it a real

date?'' He grinned shyly, and Nancy realized maybe she'd had another motive for using him as an excuse.

"We could do something fun, around nine, when I get off work?" he suggested.

"I'd love to," Nancy said, and she meant it. The dining room was crowded, and by the time her chicken salad sandwich came, it was almost seven.

"Maybe I'd better get this to go," Nancy said to Scott. "Uh, I want to do some shopping before our date."

"No problem." He removed the plate, tripping over her purse, which she'd set by her chair. The sandwich went flying, landing on the floor in a soggy heap.

He smiled sheepishly. "I'll get them to make another one—pronto."

"Leave the bill," Nancy said. She finished her drink, then left money on the bill tray. When Scott didn't return with the sandwich, Nancy went to look for him. She didn't want to be late for Weller.

She headed to the kitchen. There was a round glass window in the closed door. Peeking in, she saw Scott wrapping what looked like her sandwich. When he was finished, he tossed it in the air and, in one swift motion, caught it behind his back in a paper bag.

Nancy's eyes widened in astonishment. Minutes ago Scott had tripped over her purse. Now he was deftly juggling her dinner.

He turned toward the door, and Nancy ducked away, hurrying over to a row of potted plants. Was the clumsy guy routine for her benefit? She remembered all the times he'd threatened to knock over glasses and tip over dishes. And if so, why would he try to fool her?

"Scott!" She waved when he came out the kitchen door. "I left money on the table for the bill—and a tip," she told him.

"You can give me a tip later," he teased.

"Meet you in the lobby around nine?" she asked.

"Righto." He handed her the bag. "Enjoy. I made sure the chef prepared it specially for you."

"Thanks." Nancy waved goodbye, then sped from the restaurant.

When she reached the lobby, there was no sign of Weller. "Ms. Drew?" One of the clerks called her over to the check-in desk. "You received this message from a Detective Jackson Weller." He handed her a slip of paper.

Nancy unfolded it. "Got some important info on our cat burglar," the message said. "Meet me on the wharf in front of Harborplace."

Yes! Weller must have made a match on the prints. Excited, Nancy pushed through the revolving doors. The night air was cool and refreshing. As she walked to the wharf, she munched on half her sandwich, suddenly starved.

The walkway in front of Harborplace was crowded with Thursday night revelers. A foot-tapping trio played bluegrass music. Two mimes, their faces painted white, pantomimed climbing ladders.

While she waited, Nancy ate the last bite of sandwich, then threw the bag and wrapper away. Finished, she glanced around, wondering why Weller had wanted to meet her here. Then she spotted a whaler chugging toward the wharf, Police written in huge block letters on the center console. Maybe he was making a grand entrance by boat.

Nancy was raising her arm to wave, when she felt something cold and hard press into her ribcage. The same instant, an arm stole around her shoulders.

"Oh Nancy, I'm so glad I ran into you!" a woman gushed in her ear, the arm around her shoulder tightening as the person added in a hoarse whisper, "This time don't try to get away from me like you did at the aquarium because I'll shoot. And in this rowdy crowd, no one would even notice."

13

Cat and Mouse

What felt like a gun muzzle poked Nancy again, bruising her ribs. "Head to your right along the wharf," the woman ordered, and this time Nancy recognized the voice.

"Selena," Nancy said, imitating her fake-happy tone. "How nice to see you, too."

"Shut up," Selena retorted, "and get moving."

"Not until you tell me where we're going," Nancy said, stalling. Out of the corner of her eye, she tried to catch sight of the police boat. But it had disappeared behind a cruise ship slowly making its way to the dock.

"Look. You might have outwitted other criminals in your so-called detective career," Selena snapped. "But you're not pulling stupid stalling tricks on me."

Her cold tone sent shivers up Nancy's arm. How did Selena know Nancy was a detective? Was she the accomplice working with Chance? What else did she know?

Reluctantly, Nancy started walking to the right, her eyes scanning the crowded walkway. If only she could make a run for it. But Selena kept her arm around Nancy's shoulder as they wove through the crowds. She also kept up a constant stream of happy chatter in her ruse to make it look as if they were friends.

"I'll bet you never guessed it was me," Selena said. "All this time you've been hounding clueless Harold and stupid Karl." She snorted. "Like they had the brains to pull off countless heists."

"So you're the cat burglar's accomplice," Nancy said.

"No!" Selena's fingers dug into her shoulder like claws. "I'm not the flunky accomplice," she spat in Nancy's ear. "I *am* the cat burglar!"

Nancy gasped in astonishment. Selena gave a low chuckle of satisfaction. "Don't worry. You're not the only one I've fooled. Let me see, how many police departments are after clever little ol' me?"

"You're Chance Curran?" Nancy exclaimed.

"No way. Chance is my accomplice. Do you think I'd be stupid enough to leave fingerprints behind? Ten different heists up and down the East Coast, and the cops don't have a clue I exist. I plan on keeping it that way."

"Only they *do* know you exist," Nancy said. "They have you on videotape."

"They have George and Daniel on videotape," Selena corrected her.

"Oh, right," Nancy said, realizing Detective Weller's con had worked. George and Daniel had tricked Selena into believing they were still suspects. That meant she didn't know the police were still searching for the real burglars.

As Selena propelled her along, Nancy's mind raced to put the pieces together. Selena had been in a perfect position to frame George and Daniel. She knew what they wore, she had access to the doubloons, she knew about the pirate flags. And Nancy had never suspected her of being anything other than a publicity-hungry actress.

"If you're in the clear, why risk everything by kidnapping me?" Nancy asked.

"Because you've gotten entirely too nosy. I don't make many mistakes," Selena said, "but I did make one when I framed your friend. When I picked George for a fall guy, I didn't know you were a detective. Then when I found out you were trying to clear her, I couldn't take the chance you'd blow our plans."

"Plans?"

"Big plans. Chance and I have one last heist

before we leave the City of Pirates, and I want *you* out of the way until we've pulled it off and cleared out. So get moving."

She shoved the gun in Nancy's back, propelling her forward. Looking around, Nancy tried to get her bearings. They'd passed the science center and were heading along a darker stretch of walkway that led to rows of docks jutting into the river. Each dock had at least ten pleasure boats moored to each side.

Had Selena's accomplice been living on a boat all this time? Nancy wondered. Was it Karl? Eli? Or one of the nameless extras on the film who blended into the crowd?

"What's the big robbery you're pulling off?" Nancy asked.

Selena chuckled. "You're not getting that out of me, Drew. I've planned it too carefully. I will tell you it'll be big enough that it'll bankroll my retirement."

Nancy shrugged. "Gee, and give up such a promising acting career?"

"Oh, I don't know. I may head to Hollywood. Obviously, I've got the talent. I fooled everybody on the ship as well as that gullible Mascelli."

Mascelli. Nancy bet the reporter had a police contact and had been feeding Selena information. "Is that how you knew I was a detective?" Nancy asked.

Selena leaned so close that Nancy could smell

her perfume. "I've got so many men wrapped around my fingers, I forgot who gave me that bit of information. Still, I'll have to think about it so I can thank whoever he is."

Selena prodded her in the side. "Take a left and walk to the end of the dock. And don't try anything funny." She laughed ruefully. "Contrary to my earlier performance today, I'm a great shot."

"So you knew the pistol was loaded all the time," Nancy fumed as she headed down the dock.

"Of course. I set the whole thing up. Just like I set up every theft, planning every move so Chance and I blended into the environment. Sometimes we work at the place we hit, sometimes we work nearby. That way no one ever suspects us when we finally strike."

At the end of the dock, Nancy halted in front of a small yacht. *My Treasure* was written on the stern.

"Appropriately named, don't you think?" Selena commented. "Since we collected a boatload of treasure from those hotel rooms."

"How did you get a master key card?" Nancy asked.

"Easy," a male voice answered from the boat. "I just swiped it from the gullible manager of housekeeping."

Chance Curran! Heart thumping, Nancy stared

into the shadows. A guy stepped onto the deck of the stern, and Nancy inhaled sharply.

It was Scott Harlow.

Nancy stared at Scott, her brain numb. How could the nice guy she knew as a bumbling waiter be Chance Curran? Though, now that she saw him, it all made sense. A hotel employee would be able to find out information about guests and security as well as slip in and out of rooms without attracting too much attention. Partnered, Selena and Scott made a formidable team.

"You seem surprised," he said. He was holding a soda can. Dressed in jeans, deck shoes, and a black windbreaker, he looked like a weekend boater—not a burglar.

"I'm only surprised they let you off work early," Nancy said, her voice clear and calm though she felt anything but. No wonder he'd acted so funny and clumsy. Who would have suspected such a clown? "The restaurant was crowded."

Shrugging, he took a sip. "I told them I had an emergency."

"And that's the truth," Selena said abruptly. "We need to pull our last heist, then hightail it out of Baltimore. Get in the boat, Nancy."

Nancy hesitated. Could she make a run for it? Scream for help?

"Get in the boat," Selena repeated.

"Do what she says," Scott told her.

"Do *you* always do what she says?" Nancy asked in a mocking tone. "Because she's the boss and you're the lowly accomplice?"

"She's not my boss," Scott said, only Nancy could see the spark of anger that flared in his eyes when he glanced at Selena.

I've touched a nerve, Nancy thought. Maybe she could use his anger to her advantage.

"Cut the chatter, you two." Selena squeezed Nancy's shoulder. "This isn't a date. Get in the boat, *detective*."

She shoved Nancy in the back, sending her flying forward. Nancy landed awkwardly beside Scott, who grabbed her upper arm to steady her.

As graceful as a cat, Selena jumped into the boat beside them. "You've got the rope?"

Chance nodded toward the bow. "Coiled up front. Once we tie her up, we can stash her in the cabin."

Alarmed, Nancy cast her gaze about. She had to make a break before they tied her up. But the other boats moored on the dock were quiet and empty. And the water beyond looked cold and dark.

Behind her, at the far end of the dock, a few people still strolled along the wharf. "Don't even try it," Selena warned as if she could read Nancy's mind.

"Hurry and get that rope before she gets any stupid ideas," Selena barked.

"Yeah, do what she says, Chance," Nancy said. "After all, she's the mastermind and you're just the lackey."

"You're wrong," Chance said forcefully, but he didn't move. "We've planned every heist as a team, and we've shared everything fifty-fifty."

"You haven't shared everything," Nancy pointed out. "The evidence is all stacked against *you*. The police found your fingerprints in the hotel room. In fact, they've found them at several different heists. Selena made sure of that."

Chance glanced sharply at Selena. "You told me you'd wiped everything clean!"

"I did. Don't listen to her. Can't you tell what she's doing? She's trying to pit us against each other so she can escape." Selena jerked her head to the doorway leading into the cabin. "Forget the rope and get that duct tape. We need to seal her mouth to keep her from blabbing."

"That's right, Chance," Nancy said. "But before you do, call Selena's puppy dog, Mascelli. He obviously has a snitch in the police department. He'll tell you the truth—Detective Jackson Weller's got your prints *and* your name. You'll be the one they pin the thefts on. Selena's made sure she's never been identified."

"Shut up!" Selena roared, pushing Nancy so hard, she slammed into the wall of the cabin.

Striding across the deck, Scott grabbed Selena's wrist. "She's telling the truth, isn't she?"

"No." Selena glared at him, taking her eyes off Nancy, who saw her chance. In two strides she reached the side of the boat and, without hesitating, jumped over the stainless steel railing into the cold, murky water of the harbor.

It was so black, Nancy couldn't see a thing. Panic shot through her, but she fought it off. She had to concentrate on one thing—getting away from the boat.

Propelling herself forward with a strong kick, Nancy swam underwater until it felt as if her lungs would burst. She broke the surface, trying to keep quiet, but automatically, she gasped for air.

"I told you she was trying to escape," she heard Selena screech. "There she is!"

Frantically, Nancy pushed her wet hair from her face and glanced around. Should she swim to open harbor? Or try to hide among the boats and work her way to the wharf?

The harbor stretched in front of her like a sheet of black glass, the lights from shore reflecting mysteriously on its shimmering surface. Nancy shuddered. It was at least a mile to the other side. She might get run over by a cruise ship.

Diving again, she swam in the direction of the dock, hoping she didn't bump into something first. The water was so dark, it was impossible to see.

She surfaced beside the boat moored on the other side of *My Treasure*. The sound of feet landing heavily on the dock told her that someone was already hunting for her.

Hiding behind the other boat, she held her breath.

"You go down the dock," she heard Selena say. "We can trap her between the boats. She'll never get away."

Nancy's heart skipped a beat. She'd never make it to shore before they caught her. She'd have to head toward the open harbor.

Reaching down, she took off her shoes. Then she held on to the edge of the boat and threw them toward shore, hoping to send Selena and Chance in that direction. When she heard them splash, she dove and swam underwater away from the dock.

She was a strong swimmer, and she knew the wharf by the science center wasn't too far away. Nancy just hoped she could make it.

Nancy broke the surface, took several gulps of air, and was about to go under again when she heard the roar of a boat motor behind her.

Selena and Chance were coming after her, and there was no place to hide!

14

A Daring Rescue

Swim! Nancy told herself. Don't look back! Hand over hand she propelled herself through the cold, black water. The lights of the science center were getting closer.

But the roar of the boat was getting closer, too. Soon Nancy would be in plain sight. She didn't think Selena would hesitate to shoot.

Diving under, Nancy switched direction, hoping to lose Selena and Scott. When she came up for air, a bright light illuminated her head. "There she is!" she heard Selena shout. "Steer to the right."

Nancy filled her lungs with air and dove. But her time and her energy were running out. When she came up again, the roar of the boat was so deafening it sounded as if it was right on top of her. Then she heard another sound—the whir of a siren.

The police boat! Nancy twisted, catching sight of the flashing blue light on the whaler's center console. Selena and Chance must have spotted it, too. Their boat careened sharply and took off.

"Nancy!" Jackson Weller, dressed in a slicker, waved to her from the police boat. "I'm throwing you a life ring. Grab hold and we'll pull you to the ladder."

Nancy nodded. Her teeth were chattering, and now that she'd stopped swimming, she could feel the cold seep to her bones.

The police boat slowed, and Weller threw her a life ring attached to a rope. Holding on, Nancy kicked while Weller pulled her to the ladder mounted outside the stern.

She was trembling so hard, he had to help her up. "Put this on!" he shouted over the noise as the police boat sped up. He held out a waterproof coat with Police written on the back in white letters.

"Thank-k-k y-y-you," Nancy said, her teeth chattering. "How did you find me?"

"Karl Kidd, believe it or not. The gambler's boat was docked over on this side of the harbor. Karl said that one evening he saw Selena coming down to a boat named *My Treasure,* which was docked near the gambler's boat. When he came in to talk to us about the gambling stuff, he mentioned it."

"That was your hot tip?"

"Right. We were going to pick you up, then take you over to check out the boat, when we spotted you with Selena walking along the wharf." He grabbed hold of the railing as the police boat swerved sharply. "When I looked at the two of you through the binoculars, I could tell by your expression and actions you weren't happy to be with Ms. Ramirez."

"She had a gun on me." Nancy shuddered.

"How'd you get away?" Weller asked.

"When Chance and Selena started arguing, I jumped overboard."

"Chance?"

"Also known as Scott Harlow, a waiter at the Harborside Hotel."

"No wonder he was able to get a master key card. Selena was his accomplice?"

"No. *Selena* was the cat burglar."

Weller looked surprised for only a second. Then he shook his head.

Nancy grabbed the railing as the police boat sped up. Two officers wearing baseball caps balanced on the bow. Siren blaring, light flashing, the boat quickly drew alongside *My Treasure*. The two officers threw grappling hooks onto the deck, hooking the police boat to the yacht.

Nancy caught sight of Chance, hunched over the steering wheel in the small cabin. Selena stood in the stern, legs straddled for balance, the gun pointed at the police boat.

"Drop the gun, Ms. Ramirez," Weller shouted through a bullhorn. The police officers had drawn their guns and aimed them at her.

"Stop the boat, Curran!" Weller hollered.

Chance cut the engine, and both boats slowed to a stop. Hands raised, he came out of the cabin. "I'm unarmed," he shouted.

Selena stood firm. "Stay behind me," she snapped at him. "We're not giving up."

"Selena," Nancy called. "This isn't a movie. If you shoot someone, you'll go to jail—forever."

Selena didn't budge. Then suddenly, with an eerie wail, she dropped her arms. The gun fell to the deck. Using the grappling hook, Weller pulled *My Treasure* alongside the whaler. One officer jumped in and picked up the gun while the other kept his weapon on Selena.

"I give up!" she cried, huge tears rolling down her cheeks. "I'm so sorry. But he forced me to do everything!" Turning, she pointed a trembling finger at Chance.

Nancy thought she'd seen Selena's best performance, but this topped them all.

"He's the mastermind!" she continued to sob. "He told me if I didn't help him with the thefts, he'd ruin my acting career."

Chance was so astounded that for a second he didn't react. Then he gave a low growl and lunged for her, grabbing her around the neck.

Weller jumped into the boat and helped the

officer pull the two apart. "Cuff 'em," he barked. "Then read them their rights. I'll radio for a transport car to meet us at the dock."

Nancy pulled the coat tighter around her chest. "Nice acting, Selena," she said after the officer had handcuffed her. "Only this time, no one's clapping."

Tossing her hair behind her shoulders, Selena gave her a haughty look. "My award-winning performance is just beginning, Drew."

"I don't think a judge will be too impressed." Nancy glanced at Chance just as the officer pulled his hands behind him and snapped on the cuffs.

He gave her a lopsided smile, and for a second he looked so much like the guy she thought she knew that Nancy almost smiled back.

"You were right," he said with a resigned shrug. "After this last heist, Selena was going to throw me to the wolves to save her own skin. I'm sorry, Nancy," he added before the officer led him into the cabin.

"I'm sorry, too . . . Scott," Nancy whispered.

Selena and Chance had been as daring, cunning, and greedy as pirates, and just like the pirates of old, they'd lost in the end.

"Wow, what a story!" Harold exclaimed the next day on the *Swift Adventure*.

"Really," Andrew chimed in. "We should make it into a movie."

146

"I second that." Daniel waved one hand in the air. "I can see it on the marquee now—Andrew Wagner's *The City of Pirates* starring the famous actor Daniel Wagner."

"Just don't make me play Selena," George said, and everyone started laughing.

The cast and crew had gathered on the ship for a buffet breakfast before Friday morning's shoot. Nancy hadn't told anyone the details of Chance and Selena's arrest. She didn't have to.

The night before George, Daniel, and Andrew had met her at the police station. Joseph Mascelli was already there along with WCBN. The story had made the morning headlines and the morning news.

"Nancy, you didn't really suspect I was the cat burglar?" Eli asked for the third time.

Nancy laughed at his expectant expression. "I sure did," she told him, and everybody clapped him on the back.

She turned to Karl and Janie. "I even suspected you two when I spotted Janie after she told me she was going back to the hotel. You were following her, Karl, and both of you were traveling fast. The next instant I heard the police sirens coming from the hotel."

"Whoa." Karl rocked back on his heels. "That must have looked suspicious."

"Really suspicious after I lied to you when you asked me about it," Janie said. "But I was too embarrassed to tell you what happened. After I met you for dinner, Nancy, Karl called me at the hotel. We met on the wharf."

Karl hung his head. "I begged her to lend me money," he said. "She told me no. I was so desperate, I got a little . . . uh, insistent."

"You mean *rough*," Janie clarified. "I told him he'd been playing Blackbeard too long."

"I'm just glad you told the police about *My Treasure*," Nancy told Karl. "It saved me from a long night tied up in the cabin."

"The cops are going to go after that gambling racket, too," Karl said. "Though as long as I'm in Baltimore, I'm going to be checking over my shoulder for those goons."

Andrew threw him a pretend punch. "And we're going to be here a week longer than we thought."

Everybody turned to face him. "Why?" Lian asked. "We don't have Selena to slow us down with her million requests."

"Yes, but we do have extra footage to shoot." Andrew was grinning happily.

Nancy glanced at Daniel, who looked just as smug. "With all the publicity," Daniel explained, "we have heard from networks from all over, each wanting to buy the rights to the film. One of them, Broadcast Times, called us this morning and made us an offer. But if we go with them, they want to expand the film from a half-hour to an hour. I think Seeing Double Productions has its first hit!"

Everybody cheered, but the cheers quickly died down, and Nancy heard grumblings among the cast and crew. She couldn't blame them. Most were staying in budget hotel rooms that they were paying for out of their own pockets.

Andrew chuckled. "Oh, did we forget to tell you the best news? We've accepted Broadcast Times's offer, and it's such a good deal, you're all going to get paid!"

Hearty cheers broke out this time. Linking arms, Janie and Lian swung each other around. Harold and Eli shouted, "Better props! A new microphone!"

"What's going to happen to Selena?" Janie asked Nancy.

"Are you hoping she'll get life?" George asked.

"In a cell with no shower and makeup," Janie added while everybody laughed.

"I'm not sure what will happen," Nancy admitted. "The police are gathering evidence to build a strong case. Of course, kidnapping me will be added to her list of crimes. Plus, the two are wanted in several other cities."

"Did you ever figure out who—or what—they were planning to rob last night?" George asked. "You know, the big heist."

Nancy shook her head. "Detective Weller thinks it has something to do with the convention group that had just come into the hotel Thursday for the weekend. A lot of wealthy businesspeople and their spouses. The group is known to bring lots of jewelry and cash."

"But how did Chance and Selena know which rooms to burglarize?" Janie asked.

Harold laughed. "Really. If they'd gone into my motel room, they would've found day-old french fries."

"Chance used his job as a waiter to get friendly with the customers." Nancy sighed for a minute, realizing how good he was at duping people. "He'd chat them up, all the while finding out what their plans for the night were as well as checking out the size of their wallets. Most of them would sign the bill with their room number. Once he'd stolen the master key card, it was easy as pie."

"What I can't figure out is why Selena used the doubloons to cast suspicion on the ship," Daniel asked. "It seems so risky."

"My guess is she wanted to point the police in the direction of the ship so when the hotel got Anne Bonny and Jack Rackham on tape, they'd arrest Daniel and George. Once the police had two suspects in custody, Selena and Chance would be free to make their last heist and get out of town."

"What a smooth operation," Janie said. "And who would have thought that Selena was the mastermind."

"Not me!" Harold, Eli, and Karl chorused. "We were too busy being starstruck," Eli said.

"Speak for yourself," Daniel cut in. "I was too busy being annoyed with her acting."

George shook her head. "And to think she was actually the best actor of us all."

Andrew put his arm around Nancy's shoulder. "She fooled everybody but Nancy."

Nancy shook her head. "Wrong. She had me fooled, too. I just hope she doesn't pull the wool over the judge's and jury's eyes."

"Speaking of acting," Daniel straightened. "Who's going to play Mary Read now that Selena's in jail?"

"Nancy, of course," Karl Kidd boomed. "Anyone who can foil two real pirates can handle the role of Mary Read." Pulling a pistol from the waistband of his pants, he held it out to Nancy.

Nancy grinned. Now that the mystery had been solved, she was ready to throw herself back into the film.

Taking the pistol, she brandished it in the air. "All right, mates," she said in her best pirate's voice. "Let's get this film rolling. Before I make everybody walk the plank!"

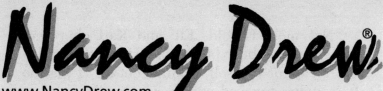

**Do your younger brothers and sisters
want to read books like yours?**

**Let them know there
are books just for *them!***

They can join Nancy Drew and her best
friends as they collect clues and solve
mysteries in

THE

NANCY DREW

NOTEBOOKS®

Starting with

#1 The Slumber Party Secret

#2 The Lost Locket

#3 The Secret Santa

#4 Bad Day for Ballet

AND

**Meet up with suspense and mystery
in The Hardy Boys® are: The Clues Brothers™**

Starting with

#1 The Gross Ghost Mystery

#2 The Karate Clue

#3 First Day, Worst Day

#4 Jump Shot Detectives

A MINSTREL® BOOK

Published by Pocket Books

The most puzzling mysteries...
The cleverest crimes...
The most dynamic
brother detectives!

The Hardy Boys®

By Franklin W. Dixon

Join Frank and Joe Hardy in up-to-date
adventures packed with action and suspense

Look for brand-new mysteries
wherever books are sold

Available from Minstrel® Books
Published by Pocket Books

2314